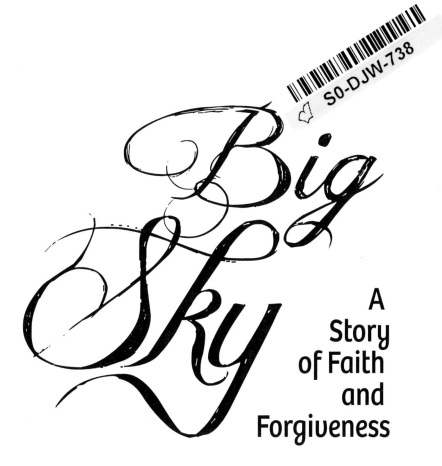

Big Sky

A Story of Faith and Forgiveness

C. J. Pagano

BOOKLOGIX®
Alpharetta, GA

ISBN: 978-1-61005-578-9

10 9 8 7 6 5 4 3 2   0 2 0 9 1 5

Printed in the United States of America

∞This paper meets the requirements of ANSI/NISO Z39.48-1992 (Permanence of Paper)

Dedicated to my husband and my two sons
for their love and support.

Brenda,
With God all things
are possible.
J. Pagano

Acknowledgments

I want to thank my family for their encouragement,
NEGA Writers Club for being an inspiration, and
my publishing team at BookLogix,
especially my editor, Kelly Nightingale.

Chapter One

Broken skis protruded from a snow mound that buried all but the shaded eyes and crimson cheeks of a champion skier. Beverly Karas lay staring at the sky above, the setting sun filtered only by her tinted goggles. Would anyone find her before she succumbed to the elements? Why did she choose late afternoon to tackle the slopes alone?

Her voice was hoarse from yelling as she tried to capture the attention of the other skiers. Beverly's effort appeared futile, so she rested her vocal cords and prayed.

Alan Wayne was making his final run of the day. He loved to catch the glow of the sun as it cast a shadow on the glistening white powder, a sight only available at sundown. Lost in thought about meeting his college friends for a late dinner, he pushed off the peak and dropped into a snowdrift. He struggled to stay upright as the snow enveloped his left ski boot, halting his momentum. He looked around for a level area providing some packed snow when he heard, "Help me."

"No, I don't care for that introduction," said author Deborah Miller as she deleted the words just entered on her laptop.

"Please place your seats in the upright position and fasten your seatbelts. We will be arriving at Bozeman Yellowstone International Airport shortly. Please refrain from using your cell phone and other electronic devices until we have landed. Thank you."

The announcement from the stewardess was welcome news as Deborah tucked the computer into her tote bag and peered out the small window to view the terrain below. The lush green forest seemed intertwined with the towering Gallatin and Madison mountain ranges.

As the plane descended, Deborah could see the old airport, Gallatin Field, had been expanded and was much larger than expected. The nearby town of Belgrade could be seen on its outskirts with houses dotted throughout the vicinity.

She deplaned and proceeded to the baggage area while ideas for exploring Big Sky, Montana, flooded her mind. Locating her luggage, she walked outside to find her ride.

This quest, yet unknown to her, would prove more memorable than any journey she had ever taken.

Chapter Two

The unusually brisk spring air caused Deborah to shiver with excitement, as it meant there should be snow on Lone Mountain.

She donned her leather jacket, her long brown hair blowing in the breeze. As she cast her eyes on the horizon, she stood awestruck at the spectacular snowcapped mountains meeting the cloudless blue sky, mirroring her vision for the cover of her new novel. Pulling a camera from her handbag, Deborah captured the view.

Glancing around anxiously, she spotted the resort van. Deborah hurried across the parking lot, dragging her resistant luggage, and stepped behind the waiting passengers. With her bags safely packed inside, she chose to sit in the rear of the van. A rather glum-looking man took the seat in front of her. His countenance was sullen, unlike the other enthusiastic travelers onboard, though there was something oddly familiar about him. His strange behavior captured her attention, and she was curious to discover the reason for his somber mood.

Leaving the airport the van traveled south on Route 85 and turned onto Route 91 toward Gallatin National Forest, where deer, elk, and moose openly grazed. The knowledgeable driver described each animal as it came into view. Deborah noticed several small boats floating on the Gallatin River. "This is great fishing country," the driver stated. After experiencing several animal sightings, everyone sat quietly for the rest of the journey. The only sounds Deborah heard were the whirring of the van's engine and an occasional comment from the driver. The peacefulness was a welcome change from the city noises she was used to hearing.

Although she missed her children and granddaughters, it was an ideal time to travel. The grandchildren were still in school, and it was a time of transition for the weather in Montana. Snow was still on the mountaintops, but the temperature was comfortable. It was her first trip alone, and she welcomed the opportunity to explore the area without distractions.

The excellent skiing and rustic resorts, pictured in many travel brochures, made it the perfect backdrop for her novel. Deborah was convinced that Big Sky would not disappoint and would give greater insight into what her characters could experience.

The driver took Route 64 toward Lone Mountain, and various signs for the area's attractions confirmed they were nearing the resort. Deborah was intrigued by the cabins dotting the rural road. She had never stayed in a log cabin and found herself lost in thought about Montana's early settlers and how they felt living in this wilderness. It must have been daring to live among the wildlife and far from civilization. The pioneers certainly didn't have the luxuries advertised by the resort she chose.

This was not the old west, she considered, but reminiscent of simpler times in America, making her feel a long way from her home in New Jersey. Deborah questioned herself as to why she had chosen such a remote part of the country to visit unaccompanied. Thinking about being alone, she felt apprehensive. It was important she dismiss those feelings, so she whispered, "God is with me, and I am protected."

She decided to ask the driver if the slopes on Lone Mountain were still open for skiing.

"There will probably be at least three more weeks of white powder on the mountain, and then the trails will be closed to skiers for the summer," he replied.

Deborah was relieved to hear she hadn't planned her trip too late in the season.

As the van turned from the main road onto a long driveway, the enormous clubhouse Deborah had seen while choosing her accommodations came into view. Though the construction reminded her of the Lincoln Logs her brother Shawn received one Christmas, she admired its authentic charm.

After retrieving her bags, Deborah registered and went directly to her suite. The rooms were fairly large, with a western décor that made it feel cozy. The couch and chair made of cordovan leather were quite comfortable, and paintings depicting western scenes hung throughout the unit. It also included a kitchenette. Deborah felt it would save time to have breakfast in her room, leaving more opportunity for recording her thoughts.

From the bedroom window, Deborah caught her first glimpse of Lone Mountain in the distance. It was more majestic than depicted in the photos viewed online. Deborah couldn't detect anyone skiing but noticed the snow that blanketed the peak. Her plan was to experience the mountain and its surroundings the following day. Viewing the peak up close was paramount in exploring Big Sky.

A once-avid skier, Deborah planned for her characters to meet while skiing, and Lone Peak was known for having some of the best trails for seasoned professionals. It provided the romantic setting she was looking for, and it was the regional atmosphere that drew her to the area. Her only disappointment was an old knee injury that prevented her from enjoying the slopes firsthand.

Exhausted from the plane ride and hour-long journey from the airport, Deborah was relieved to stretch across the four-poster bed. Its sturdy timber construction and comfy mattress made her feel like Goldilocks—it was just right. The idea of spending the evening snuggled under the plush down comforter was appealing, but her stomach began to growl. It was time to find the nearest restaurant. The clubhouse was convenient, and since she hadn't made arrangements to stock the kitchenette, it was about her only option.

Deborah showered and chose to wear a figure-flattering, navy blue A-line dress. Throughout her life she had been heavyset, but after her husband's death, she lost an immense amount of weight. Now her demeanor radiated confidence. She strolled through the lobby to the restaurant, where the hostess greeted her with a welcoming smile and seated her near the entrance. Her table provided a view of the entire room, perfect for observing the individuals dining at the lodge.

Deborah loved people watching. She wondered what interesting characters Big Sky would produce. She frequently used those she observed in her writing—visualizing them as actors in an ongoing play. It was great fun, and they were unaware of her intention.

The waiter offered her a menu then filled her glass with water, and placed it on the table. She ordered a cup of coffee, knowing the caffeine would help revive her. Deborah smiled as she read the menu that included caribou chops and buffalo tenderloin. It was certainly unlike the cuisine served at the restaurants she frequented. Not feeling adventurous, she ordered a petite sirloin steak.

While slowly sipping her steaming coffee, Deborah's eyes searched for subjects to examine. Suddenly, she felt conspicuous being alone and, with her choice of evening attire, decidedly less casual than her fellow diners.

Since the situation couldn't be changed, she passed the time by making mental notes of the restaurant décor, while continuing to investigate its characters. A couple in the corner must be newlyweds, she thought. They held hands across the table, and their eyes were transfixed—reminding her of the early years with Ryan. Sadly, the affection in her own marriage had faded over time, and she envied the apparent passion between the young couple. It seemed impossible that five years had passed since Ryan's fatal heart attack.

The realization of dining alone made Deborah miss her family, but she knew it wouldn't be good to dwell on those feelings—there was work to do.

The waiter served her entrée, "Will you need anything else?"

"I don't believe so, thank you."

The restaurant was crowded as Deborah continued to scan the room. A baby fussing, a family celebrating a birthday, two men presumably having a business dinner, but over in the corner near the entrance to the kitchen, she spied the man from the van. He was slumped over his coffee and still appeared forlorn. *Why was he downcast in such a marvelous place?* After a few minutes, Deborah watched as he stood and exited the door nearest her.

Usually sweets were not included in Deborah's diet, but when the waiter rolled a cart of scrumptious-looking desserts past her table, her taste buds were tempted, and she ordered the strawberry cheesecake. Feeling refreshed, she was anxious to return to her room and begin the task that had brought her to Montana. Deborah paid the bill, thanked the waiter for his excellent service, and walked down the corridor to her suite.

She planned to spend her evening jotting down the sights and sounds she had already encountered, but first, she needed to phone her daughter Megan. When she got a voice recording, Deborah left a message, "Sorry I missed you, just wanted you to know I made it to Big Sky. Please call me back."

There was still an hour or two of daylight—enough time to record her observations. Deborah slipped out of her blue dress and changed into a sweatshirt and jean skirt. She picked up her cell phone and slid it into her jacket pocket, grabbed her laptop, and stepped out of the sliding glass door to the patio. Trying to close the screen door, she pulled it off its track. "Oh, no, how am I going to fix this?"

"Hello, may I help?" Deborah was stunned by a voice coming from the adjoining patio. It was the downcast man from the van. His slight grin was appealing, and she noticed strands of silver throughout his well-groomed auburn hair. "My name is Will. I'd be glad to help you with the door. It's what I do."

"Are you an employee here?"

"No, I'm not. Home improvement is my business, though. I'm familiar with doors, tracks, and hinges."

Deborah recognized a southern drawl in his reply. "Great, please help me. By the way, I'm Deborah Miller."

"It's good to meet you, Deborah. Now, let's see about fixing the door." Will opened the adjoining gate and took a few steps to the doorway. Pulling a Swiss Army knife from his jacket, he made a few small adjustments, and the door slid smoothly.

"Thank you, you're a godsend. I wish I had something to offer you. My kitchen isn't stocked yet."

"Would you like some ice tea? I'm in the adjoining suite."

"No, thank you," Deborah said with trepidation.

"Would you drink some if I brought the glasses to the patio?"

Deborah blushed. "Was it that obvious?"

"It's refreshing to see a woman with scruples."

As Will left to get the tea, Deborah felt it wasn't beneficial chatting with this stranger when she needed to be concentrating on her notes.

Will appeared carrying two tall glasses. Typing on her computer, Deborah lifted her head as Will placed the glasses on the patio table. "The tea looks delightful."

"Aren't you here to rest and relax? You look like someone on a mission," Will said rather smugly.

"Actually, it's not a vacation for me. This is a working assignment. I'm a writer; I'm here for research and inspiration."

"You can't work in this paradise. You need to embrace its nature and really explore what it has to offer."

Bewildered by his comments, Deborah was becoming irritated. *How could he say those things when he didn't seem to be enjoying himself?* He was helpful with the door, so she decided not to be disagreeable.

"This is a lovely place," she replied.

"Then why not enjoy it?"

"It's important to have my outline and research done this week. My deadline is in three months, and there's so much more to compile."

"Do you have ten minutes or less to drink your tea?"

"You're right; ten minutes won't hurt." She could chalk it up to research if she could elicit Will's story. With the laptop set aside, Deborah sipped the tea. "This is delicious."

"I made it myself. We in Georgia make great sweet tea."

"So you're from Georgia. Where do you live?"

"I live in a town north of Atlanta called Alpharetta."

Deborah continued, "And you work in a home improvement store?"

"You might say that. Well, I own three stores in the Atlanta area."

"What brings you to Big Sky?"

Will became silent, just when he seemed to be receptive to Deborah's questioning. "I don't mean to pry but you seem a little withdrawn."

He paused and said, "It's this place."

"You just gave me the impression you love Big Sky."

"I've come back this week to confront my past."

"What do you mean?" Deborah thought she would finally discover what was troubling him.

"Deborah, I'm sorry, but it's just too difficult to talk about."

"It might help to express whatever is bothering you. I'm a good listener."

With a hesitating sigh he began, "My wife and I loved to come here to fish and relax from our business. She died two years ago. I'm trying to deal with her loss and other family problems. I thought coming to reminisce would help, but it's only made me feel lonelier."

"Will, I apologize for prying. If I can do anything for you, please let me know."

"Thank you. I need to leave now." He pushed away from the table, stood, and reached for the empty glasses.

"I understand. Thank you for the tea."

Will nodded as he turned and walked away.

How awful her motive had been, she considered. She was looking for writing material, and he was genuinely depressed. It was difficult to concentrate on the outline, so Deborah went inside. As she passed through the door, she was reminded how considerate Will had been. She turned on the radio but couldn't find anything to suit her taste. Her mind was preoccupied with Will; there was something peculiar about him.

The phone in her suite rang, and Deborah rushed to answer it. She thought it must be one of her children calling. She lifted the receiver and said, "Hi there."

"Deborah, is it you?"

"Who is this?"

"It's Will from next door."

Deborah felt terrible for the way she cheerfully answered the phone. "Oh, Will, yes it's me."

"Were you serious about helping me?"

She was wondering what she had gotten herself into, but slowly replied, "Yes, what do you need?"

"I really hate to eat alone. Will you have breakfast with me at the clubhouse?"

Deborah thought she owed him that much. "Of course, Will, I'll meet you in the lobby at 8:00 a.m., if that's all right with you?"

"That's just fine, thank you."

Although she had an uncanny feeling they had met before, Deborah wondered why she involved herself with Will. She convinced herself it would only be for breakfast. The stores wouldn't be open at that hour, and she did have to eat. After breakfast she wouldn't feel obligated to him. She would make it clear she would be working for the remainder of her stay.

Chapter Three

The next morning, Will was waiting in the lobby. He was impeccably dressed in khaki slacks and a brown striped shirt. His graying auburn hair and glasses made him appear quite distinguished. The handyman from yesterday was quite captivating. He definitely reminded her of someone. Not knowing many people from Georgia, she dismissed the thought.

"Good morning, Deborah. You look lovely."

"Thank you for inviting me to breakfast. I insist we go Dutch." Will's expression turned to a smug frown. Why did this man make her feel so uncomfortable? It had become annoying.

"Did you get much written on your book last night?"

"No, I must have been tired from the trip." She didn't want to tell him how moved she was by the poor man having difficulty dealing with his wife's death.

She remembered how her life changed following her husband's passing. Many mornings she made a full pot of coffee then realized Ryan wasn't there for breakfast. Before his death, Deborah drank coffee with her husband every morning. She recognized it was the cherished time of sitting with him in their sunroom before he rushed off to work that she had enjoyed.

Deborah didn't miss the dinners, parties, and many social functions connected with Ryan's business. His colleagues seemed so shallow and weren't really her friends; they were associates of Ryan. They seemed to forget she was still living now that he was gone. Deborah was glad her church family hadn't abandoned her. Now she filled her days with writing and working for the church. Although her children were available when she needed them, if it hadn't been for the Lord, returning to a normal life would have been difficult. Yes, she understood what Will must be going through.

Deborah and Will walked down the corridor to the restaurant, and a hostess showed them to a table near a large bay window. After they were seated, Deborah engaged in small talk to begin her interrogation of Will. She was anxious to know who he really was. Other than knowing he owned his own business and lost his wife, Deborah didn't know very much about this stranger.

"So you were born in Georgia?"

"No, I was born in Pennsylvania and settled in Georgia after my tour in the military."

The waiter interrupted to suggest they try the resort special plate, and she didn't hear Will's reply. Deborah's questioning of him missed the most important fact, his birth state—a fact that would reveal his true identity.

They both took the waiter's suggestion and ordered the Resort Special. When it was served, the large platter filled with eggs, bacon, waffles, and home fries was much more than Deborah anticipated. "I'll have to walk several miles to work off all the calories."

"Nonsense, it will give you the energy needed to deal with the demanding terrain here in the mountains."

"My eyes were bigger than my stomach. Though I must say, it is quite good."

Will asked Deborah, "How did you discover Big Sky?"

"A friend knew how much we enjoyed skiing and told us about the locale several years ago. When I chose to write about skiers, it seemed to have the perfect combination of rustic charm and difficult slopes. I concentrated on the area around the resort for my research, but if you could suggest some local sites that might enhance my story, I would appreciate the help," Deborah said.

"This place has a lot to offer—the lakes, wildlife, and Yellowstone nearby. There is so much you can see and do; I find something new each time I visit."

It seemed like the years of sheltering herself from a man's attention were forgotten. She felt comfortable in his presence and enjoyed talking with someone who knew so much about Montana.

As they finished eating, Will said, "If you'd like, I can drive you to town to buy your groceries. I want to buy a newspaper and get a few other items."

Deborah hesitated in replying. How could she decline his offer? Her mind wandered.

"Deborah, did you hear me? Would you like to go to town with me?"

How could she say no? Under any other circumstance, his invitation would be welcome. He was trying to be pleasant; it certainly wasn't his appearance making her hesitate. After much insistence, she reluctantly gave in to him. "Sure Will, give me a few minutes to get my shopping list."

They were unaware of the surprise awaiting them in town.

Chapter Four

The scenery was breathtaking as Deborah and Will drove to the village stores. She could appreciate the reason Big Sky was Will's favorite place to relax. Massive trees lined the highway, and the winding mountain passes were spectacular. The mountains appeared to have rivers of snow flowing down from the upper slopes.

Deborah asked, "How long have you been coming to Big Sky?"

"More than ten years. Except for the past two years; I couldn't bear the idea of coming here without my wife."

"You must have had a good marriage."

"Sherry and I were extremely close. She was not only my wife and best friend, but also my business partner and bookkeeper. Now I have an accountant. My life has changed quite a bit in a short time. Enough about me," said Will. "Why did you decide to be a writer?"

"It's been my passion since I was very young; I would compose stories about unusual people and exotic places. I love doing research; discovering little known facts of different regions invigorates me. I've only had one of my stories published, but it was good enough for an advance on a second. I suppose I didn't really take my writing seriously until my husband died."

"Then you are a widow?"

"Yes, it's been five years. My husband had a heart attack."

"So you do know what it's like to lose your best friend."

"I'm not sure about that; I had a good marriage, but we were so busy socializing we had little time for each other. I kept busy with my children and church activities during the day. Ryan was a workaholic and rarely at home, unless it was to dress for a business party. We were at the same functions, but it usually turned into a business meeting for him while I was with the neglected wives."

Realizing how negative she sounded, Deborah added, "It wasn't quite as bad as it sounds: the wives were friendly, and it was always a good time to catch up on the latest news. Very few of us spoke on a regular basis, and I haven't seen most of them for several years."

Deborah continued, "Ryan had taken care of our property and other financial matters. It was quite a challenge for me at first. Writing kept me sane. I really enjoy what I do. I can dictate my own schedule and allow time for those I love, my obligations, and activities."

"Where do you call home?"

"New Jersey, we live just off exit 5 on the New Jersey Turnpike in Mount Holly."

"You said we, how many children do you have?"

"I have three children, one daughter and two sons. They all live within fifteen miles of my home. I don't think I would want it any other way."

As they neared the Big Sky Town Center, Deborah gazed at the eye-catching wooden and stone façade of the stores. What a difference from the shopping centers at home, she observed. Most of the buildings were connected and had the same wood and stone construction. *It is just perfect for my book*, she contemplated.

Will parked near the Hungry Moose grocery store, and a car pulled beside them. A man jumped out and knocked at Will's window. Glancing at a rather short man wearing a fishing hat and plaid shirt, his face hidden by Will's torso, Deborah felt sure it was no one she knew. Will yelled, "Rev. Benning, what are you doing here?" It surprised Will to see his pastor in Big Sky.

"I thought you knew I took your suggestion about vacationing here. Mom and I are staying in a cabin on the lake. It's great fishing country." Robert Benning noticed the female in the car with Will and lifted his hat when Will shifted upright to introduce his pastor to Deborah. Rev. Benning looked across the front seat to see a rather shocked look on Deborah's face. She recognized his voice and then those familiar chubby cheeks and bright blue eyes, "Why Debby Cantrell, what are you doing here with Will?"

Will's face turned pale, and Deborah noticed a slight smirk. What had she done?

"Hello, Robert, it's good to see you. How's Susan?"

"Oh, she's fine. She won't believe I've seen you two, and together. How did this happen?"

"No, Robert, you are mistaken. Will and I just met; we're staying at the same resort. He brought me to buy my supplies."

Robert smiled as his eyebrows lifted. "Mom will want you both to come for dinner, and you'd better not disappoint her. Sorry I can't stay and chat; she'll scold me if I don't get back with her packages. I'll call you later." Rev. Benning got into his car and disappeared down the road.

"I suppose we have dinner plans," Deborah said.

"Why did Robert call you Debby Cantrell?" Will appeared guarded in his question.

"It was my maiden name. Robert went to Bible College with my brother."

"Deborah, my name is William 'Billy' Dougherty."

Deborah was stunned by his disclosure. "What! You're from Georgia. You can't be Billy. You even have a southern accent."

"I live in Georgia now, but I told you this morning I was born in Pennsylvania."

"Now I know why you never told me your last name. You had recognized me."

"No! It was only when Rev. Benning spoke your name that I knew. You looked much different, and a bit younger, the last time I saw you."

"You reminded me of someone, but you're different with your graying hair and glasses. This changes everything."

"What do you mean?"

"Well, for one thing, Robert thinks we just met."

"Is it terrible to meet again, Deborah?"

"I'm sorry. It's amazing to find the man I've been feeling sorry for was once my best friend."

"I am just as surprised as you are. You were the last person in the world I thought I would meet here."

"It's been such a long time, almost forty years. How is it possible?"

"Yes, we're definitely different; I honestly didn't recognize you. We were very young, and as I recall, you had a habit of breaking up with me at least once a year. It's amazing how we remained friends for several months then we'd start dating again. What a wonderful, innocent time it was. Why did you break up with me?"

"You never knew the reason? It sounds a bit childish now, but my mother always told me not to accept gifts from those who couldn't afford them. I broke up with you from November until Valentine's Day so you wouldn't buy me any presents. I knew your mother was a single parent, and I didn't want you to feel obligated to spend money on me. I felt terrible the first Christmas we went steady when I heard you bought me a giant teddy bear. I even told your friend Andy you should give it to your sister when I secretly wanted it for myself."

"Deborah, I never understood." Will threw his head back and laughed. "My mother thought you treated me horribly."

There was an awkward silence, and then Will reached his arm around Deborah's neck and drew her toward him. He kissed her on the cheek and then realized Deborah's resistance. "I'm sorry. I was touched by the story." He bounced his head on the headrest. "I never knew why. Thank you, Deborah. After all these years, to find out you were just being thoughtful. I cared enough for you to take the personal hurt. Boy, I never put the dates together. My sister wanted to scratch your eyes out for the way you treated me."

"If I hadn't moved, maybe things would have turned out differently. I went to Pitt and you went into the military."

"It's strange how our lives went in separate directions, and now we're together again. Deborah, do you believe God brought us to this place? That He used Big Sky to reunite us?"

"I know He directs my life. I never knew you to be religious."

"How do you think I know Rev. Benning? He's my pastor."

"This was not what I was expecting when I came here," Deborah said still in disbelief. "I need some time to consider what just happened." Deborah opened the car door and entered the store, thoughts of what just transpired swirling in her head. *Why now, Lord? This was just to be a working mission.* Deborah was baffled, wondering how she had not recognized Billy. It was understandable—their looks changed over the years—but it seemed impossible they didn't recall one another.

After making her purchases, she took the bags to the car. The door was unlocked, and she placed the packages in the back seat. Will had gone to one of the other stores. When he returned, he started the car and asked Deborah if there was anywhere else she needed to go. Deborah just sat, reflecting where this new disclosure could lead.

"Are you okay?" Will saw a look of confusion in her eyes.

Her answer was short and sweet. "Just fine, let's return to the resort." Deborah wasn't sure how to deal with this disclosure. It didn't make sense to be sitting with Billy and not know him. The old feelings for him overwhelmed her, and she was caught in the turmoil of how, after all these years, Billy was back in her life. They had severed ties long ago, or at least she felt they had. Remembering the years it took to overcome her heartbreak, she didn't want those feelings revived.

Neither one spoke as they drove to the resort. It was strange to have such silence between them. It made Deborah recall the time Billy got his first car. He was taking her home from a party, and they sat speechless the entire way. They would talk for hours on the phone and at school, but the idea of being alone together in a car made them both uneasy.

The reunion was a total shock. Just because they had feelings years ago didn't mean those feelings still existed, Deborah thought.

When they finally arrived at the resort, Deborah thanked Will for the ride, grabbed the grocery bags, and hurried toward her door. Will followed behind until she stopped and struggled to find her passkey. "Here, let me hold your bags," he said. Reluctantly, she pushed them into his arms. Deborah opened the door and reached for the bags, but he wouldn't release them. She turned and walked to the kitchenette.

Will placed the bundles on the counter and said, "So, old friend, is this it?"

"What do you mean?"

"Deborah, I'm too old for guessing games; I certainly can't read your mind. Maybe I should leave."

Deborah walked to the front door and opened it. "Sorry, I just can't cope with this right now."

Will stepped into the hallway, and Deborah closed the door. She lost him years ago, and she never wanted those feelings revived. Tears welled up, and she found herself giving into them. Throwing herself across the bed, Deborah lay crying about the past. She had once loved Billy more than anyone. He hadn't understood how devastated she was when he began dating other girls just to make her jealous. When he sent a letter from boot camp asking her to write, Deborah had found it too painful to answer. She didn't want him to know how wounded she felt, so there was no communication between them.

Now he was back, if only for a few days, and Deborah soothed herself with the fact this was a different man; a man who had been married for many years to a woman he seemed to adore. He was a changed man with a business, a family, and even different in appearance.

Suddenly, she remembered leaving the bagged food on the kitchen counter. She was too old to be acting this way. While putting her purchases away, the suite phone rang. Disguising how miserable she felt, she answered slowly, "Hello."

"Deborah, are you okay? Rev. Benning said dinner will be at seven tonight."

"Will, I can't. Do not ask me why. Just go without me."

"They're expecting both of us."

"Please give them my regrets." Deborah hung up the phone. Would Susan understand? Deborah really wanted to see her. It had been a year since the Bennings attended her brother's church dedication, and she spent so little time with Susan then.

The phone rang again. It was a woman's voice. "It's Susan. Will said you weren't up to coming for dinner. Honey, you must come. I'm anxious to see you."

"Susan, I'm sorry. Forgive me."

"No excuses. Will is glad to bring you. I won't take no for an answer. See you soon."

Why had Will phoned Susan? Now she was forced to go. So much for her plans to see the mountain, although she felt too miserable to enjoy it anyway. There would be nothing to hinder her from going tomorrow; she was determined not to put her plans on hold.

At six thirty, Will knocked on the door. She opened it to find the man she loved so long ago staring into her reddened eyes.

"You've been crying."

"Yes, I thought I had dealt with my feelings for you years ago." Will pulled her toward him. He put his arms around her neck and held her close to him. Deborah pulled away abruptly. "I'm sorry, Billy, or I mean, Will."

"What is it?"

"Nothing!"

"Tell me what is wrong?"

"Will, don't you remember how we felt about each other?"

"Yes, but you didn't write me when I left, so I thought you decided to move on with your life."

"I couldn't bring myself to accept that you would date other people and expect me to wait for you."

"What do you mean?"

"You dated several girls trying to make me jealous, and it crushed me."

"My sister insisted I should date others because you were always breaking up with me. She didn't like to see me hurt. I felt awful treating you that way."

After a brief silence, Deborah sighed. "Will, I'm such an idiot. God brought us together, and I haven't been allowing His will in this. Forgive me for being insensitive."

"The Bennings are waiting for us. I know Susan wants to see you."

"Give me just a minute." Deborah left to wash her face and comb her hair. When she reappeared, Will held the door of the suite for her and reached for her hand as they walked to the car. Hesitating before opening the passenger door, he bent forward, peering into her eyes. "Deborah, God knew I would need you here to confront the past. He knew I was running from any attempt at real happiness and hiding myself in my work."

Deborah looked at him tenderly. "Yes, writing about life, not really living it, has been my hiding place."

Chapter Five

Will and Deborah pulled up to the cabin and saw Susan in the doorway. Deborah had always admired Susan. The first time they met was the week before the Bennings' wedding. Deborah was much younger than Susan and Robert.

Robert was an only child who had spent most of his time at the Cantrell's home during college breaks; he treated Deborah like a little sister. When Robert was engaged, he insisted that "his little sis" be their flower girl. Susan made Deborah feel so important, and their wedding was one of her fondest memories. Susan was the prettiest bride Deborah had ever seen.

Susan had aged well, still attractive, her former blonde hair now snow white. Deborah was glad she insisted they come for dinner.

"Deborah, how great to see you," Susan said as she hugged her. "I'm glad you didn't disappoint me." Robert stood behind Susan with his hand extended for Will to shake. "Excellent suggestion Will; this place is fantastic. Mom and I are really getting the rest we needed. Now come inside, dinner is almost ready."

Deborah followed Susan into the kitchen, while Will and Robert relaxed in the living room. Staring at Deborah, Susan said, "There is a peace about you. Will said you weren't feeling very well. You certainly look fine. What was he talking about?"

"Susan, it's a long story."

"We'll have all night. You can tell me later. The men are probably starving." Susan picked up some bowls and walked into the dining room. "Please come to the table," she announced.

As they ate, Deborah noticed Susan staring at Will. "So you two have just met?" Deborah knew it was time to tell them the whole story. "Will and I didn't just meet. We went to school together and went 'steady' during those years, to use an old cliché. When he went into the military, we didn't keep in touch."

Will continued, "If it hadn't been for meeting Robert, we may never have been aware of our true identities."

"That's just amazing. God works in mysterious ways," Robert said.

Susan giggled. "Will looks happier than I've seen him in years." Deborah knew what she meant.

"Do you think God is trying to tell you something?" Robert said with a dimpled grin.

"We know our reunion is for a purpose, but it's been a long time, and I'm sure we have changed a great deal," answered Will.

"We don't want to rush into anything," Deborah added.

They talked and laughed about old times, and the evening quickly passed.

"We should be going," said Will. Deborah nodded in agreement. They said their good-byes, and Deborah promised to see the Bennings again before they left Montana. As Will held the car door open, Deborah slid into the passenger seat. He smiled at her as he shut the door, and she knew why she hadn't recognized him. He hadn't smiled. There was no denying who he was when he smiled—his eyes glowed and he beamed from within. This was the Billy she remembered.

They both waved good-bye to the Bennings as Will pulled out of the driveway.

Deborah knew her life was about to change. She felt her face flush. Here they were again, driving alone in his car. It felt absurd to think that way.

Will reached across the console and squeezed her hand. "Deborah, can we please spend the time we have in Big Sky to renew our friendship? There are so many places I'd like to show you."

"I was just thinking this would make a good book," chuckled Deborah. "You have to give me at least tomorrow at Lone Mountain to gather some facts. I need to get a sense of the slopes on Lone Peak and the local atmosphere; then we'll spend the remainder of the week getting reacquainted." Deborah knew she would gain additional knowledge of the area by enjoying its surroundings with Will.

When they arrived at the resort, Will walked Deborah to her door and kissed her gently on the lips. "I'll see you at eight o'clock for breakfast, and then we'll drive to the base of the mountain. Did you know you can go to the summit?"

"In one of the brochures I read a tram will take you there."

"Yes, it's worth the trip. Hope you aren't afraid of heights. I'll see you in the morning."

Deborah was preparing for bed when the phone rang. "Mom, where have you been? I thought you would be in your room early. You had me terrified."

"I forgot to take my cell phone. I met Robert and Susan Benning here, and we had dinner at their cabin tonight. I'm sorry I made you worry."

Deborah felt it was too soon to explain meeting Will. Tomorrow would be the beginning of a new chapter in her life. She would wait for just the right time to share the news with her children.

After the phone call, Deborah picked up her bible and read a passage she was very familiar with—Psalm 126:5. "They that sow in tears shall reap in joy." She smiled, thinking how it had a different meaning to her—the day had begun with tears but ended with such joy.

Chapter Six

Deborah was excited at the prospect of ascending Lone Peak. The mountain vista from her room was imposing, and she knew reaching the top would be spectacular. The research for her book was turning out to be quite an adventure.

Big Sky was exactly the background Deborah envisioned for her novel, the ambiance was a perfect fit for her characters. The small resort area was the premier destination for ski lovers. It offered some of the most challenging slopes anywhere.

As they drove toward Mountain Village, Deborah's heart began pounding in anticipation of the trip on the tram. Her only disappointment was being unable to ski its demanding slopes.

They bought their tickets and waited for their turn to make the ascent. Only those with exceptional skiing ability entered the tram with the sightseers. It was the only way to make the trip to the ridge on Lone Peak.

Of the three ski trails from the summit, two were skill-rated the highest possible—double black diamond. The other, Liberty Bowl, was considered a single diamond but only recommended for the expert skier.

Will recounted, "The tram has been popular with tourists, and skiers who just want to enjoy the view. There have already been a few changes to the tram since it opened. Originally, the inside was painted pink to calm the riders, or so they said. They must have realized if you're going to have a problem with the height and being dangled in the air, it doesn't matter what color it's painted inside. The artwork on the outside was also added later."

As they entered the tram, a young man carrying his skis stood near Deborah. He was fidgety and extremely pale. Looking out the window, Deborah could see the cable in front of them. It was the only thing holding them, and the ground was growing farther away. For a brief moment Deborah found it unnerving.

Will pointed to the area called the "Bowl." It was a scooped-out area in the center of the peak. Many skiers could be seen on its less demanding slopes. Deborah was enjoying the ride but was intrigued with the young man next to her. He seemed extremely nervous, shifting from side to side. "Is this your first time skiing the mountain?"

"No, I've skied the peak many times. It's a little frightening at first. Just looking down at the Bowl gives me second thoughts, but the moment I take that lunge downward, it's the most euphoric feeling ever. I guess the exhilaration keeps me coming back."

"Do you ever wonder why you feel the necessity to take the risk?"

"Yes, but when you've made it down the first time, the other slopes don't give you the same rush."

It was a clear day as they reached the top, and Deborah couldn't believe her eyes. The valley below with the mountains in the distance was spellbinding. Will told her they were viewing three states and two National Parks from their vantage point. A sign caught her eye; it read that going beyond the area could result in death. Skiing from this elevation was not for the fainthearted.

Deborah told the young skier to have a good run and silently whispered a prayer for his safety as he exited the tram.

Excited and inspired by the experience to the top of Lone Peak, Deborah was a little disappointed as the tram made the turn for its descent. She watched with envy as a few skiers descended the trail under the tram. Will explained that "Big Couloir," the name of the trail, was the most difficult of the three trails available from the peak. Thoughts of her characters' pleasure maneuvering downhill engaged Deborah's imagination, and she wrote mentally until the tram reached the bottom. Will also told her that several weddings were held on the tram. A wedding on the peak could be an interesting ending for her book, she thought.

Afterward, they stopped at the resort built by the former newscaster Chet Huntley. Deborah enjoyed seeing the large bear statue in the lobby while they walked to the lounge for a late lunch.

A man walked toward their table, and Will stood up and said, "Hi, Harry. I didn't think I would see you on this trip." Will turned to Deborah and introduced Harry Walker, a local realtor.

"It's nice to meet you, Deborah. How did you ever get involved with this man?"

Deborah smiled, explaining how she met Will at the resort. It was clear Will had known Mr. Walker for some time, and she didn't want him to feel awkward.

"Will, I have some great real estate to show you."

"I'm really not interested in buying anything at this time."

"Why don't you at least let me show you the new cabins we've built? I know Deborah would love them. Most women are wowed by the views."

Deborah was enthused. "Will, it might be fun to see them." It would be good for her research to see how some of the natives lived.

Harry insisted, "We can go now if you'd like. The views at sundown are stunning."

Will gave into his persistence and said they would join him.

Harry held the back door of his Navigator for Deborah, and Will sat in the front passenger seat. Mr. Walker asked Will, "Why have you changed your mind about a place in Montana? You spend so much time here."

"It just doesn't hold the same fascination for me anymore."

"With the way you enjoy fishing?"

"Yes, but I may not make as many trips as I have in the past, and it wouldn't be worth investing in a cabin I don't use."

"I can always rent it out for you, if you're interested," said Harry.

They pulled to the front of the first cabin, and Deborah wasn't very impressed. There was nothing special about the façade. It was just the usual log cabin. She was wondering if the trip was a waste of time. Harry pointed out its features, but neither Will nor Deborah was interested.

The second cabin had an unusual walkway made of stone and wood. Its large cathedral windows were more than two stories high. Deborah walked through the immense wooden double doors into a large foyer. She continued down a long hallway that led to an enormous game room with a cathedral window framing the vista of Lone Mountain. There was no way she could possibly afford this magnificent showpiece, but the allure of the summit was mesmerizing. She found herself, for the first time in her life, desiring something she had no possible way of possessing.

Harry could see the radiance in Deborah's eyes as she gazed out the window. "Beautiful sight," declared Harry. Deborah could only shake her head in agreement. Will just smiled at her childlike, dreamy state. Will told Harry they had seen enough and needed to return to the restaurant to get his car.

After saying their good-byes, Will walked Deborah to the car. "You really liked the second cabin didn't you?"

"Yes, but there's no way I can afford it, and I wouldn't come here enough to enjoy it. I'm not sure my children would ever travel to Big Sky." Deborah was a little disappointed hearing herself verbalize the truth.

"It was nice but impractical for a widow," Will teased.

Reaching the resort, Will said, "Tomorrow we'll drive to Yellowstone. Old Faithful is only a couple of hours from here." Will reached for her chin. Drawing it to him, he pressed his lips against hers.

Deborah looked into his eyes and smiled, "I'm looking forward to it; I'll pack a lunch."

She closed the door to her suite, feeling like a teen again. It was difficult to concentrate, but she knew she must transcribe her notes before retiring. When she finally climbed into bed, thoughts of the day and its perfect ending kept her awake until after midnight. She wondered how long this bliss would last.

Chapter Seven

Will knocked at Deborah's door, and she looked through the peephole to see him grinning. Opening the door, she greeted him. "Good morning, handsome."

"Are you ready for our adventure to Yellowstone? It is a fascinating place."

"I've been looking forward to seeing the park ever since you mentioned it. It didn't occur to me to include it in my itinerary. To be this close and not see it would be a terrible oversight."

"I'm glad you have allowed me to share the area with you. I thought you were a stranger just a few days ago, but I'm glad we reconnected. I know God has been at work."

"Will, we still need to take it slow. You were here to deal with feelings for your wife. I don't want to be just a temporary replacement."

"You aren't. I believe God brought us together. You should too."

"People do change, Will. What if we aren't compatible?"

"Let's just take the time to find out."

Though she enjoyed being with Will, Deborah had gotten accustomed to being single and wasn't sure if she wanted to alter her life, which was so comfortable and safe.

The mountains were a glorious setting for this special time. Deborah felt surrounded by God's presence. Everything was happening so fast. Will seemed to have dropped the mantle of gloom he was wearing the day they first met. It was a miracle they'd found each other, but Deborah didn't know if she was ready to have another man in her life. The fact that all the pieces fit like a puzzle and could only be by God's design gave her an inner peace.

Will was quite talkative, pointing out several interesting sites along the way. Deborah had a small notebook to jot down some of the places Will mentioned. It was evident he had vast knowledge of the area.

Arriving in Yellowstone, they entered through the west entrance. When they got to Madison, they turned right toward the visitor center near the Old Faithful Inn. Deborah was awed by the steam emanating skyward from the eruption of Old Faithful across from the parking area. She was anxious to see it close-up.

They were thirsty from the long ride, so Will suggested they stop at the inn for a cup of coffee before their hike past the geysers. It gave them time to recoup from the drive.

As they entered the inn, the huge fireplace, the sixty-five-foot ceiling, and the upper floor balcony rails made of crooked pine impressed Deborah.

They walked to the dining room with its ambiance of a log cabin. The frames of the stately chairs were made from large tree branches with cane backs and seats. Will suggested they order the baked brie appetizer. It was a specialty of the inn and a favorite of his.

As they sat sipping their coffee and enjoying the puffed pastry which came with the brie, Will reached across the table, taking Deborah's hand. "Deborah, I want to thank God for bringing you back into my life. The Lord knew what I needed. I needed you."

A tear fell from her cheek, and he gently brushed it away.

"It has been a wonderful reunion for me as well. If I'm dreaming don't wake me."

They lingered for several moments in the pleasure of each other's company, then Will told her it would be a long walk to view all the geysers he wanted to show her; they needed to begin their journey.

From the porch of the inn, Deborah could see the first stop on the walking tour over the bubbling hot ground beneath a walkway known as the "boardwalk." Deborah enjoyed the anticipation of the eruption of Old Faithful. The odor was quite foul, due to the sulfur, but it was an experience Deborah didn't want to miss.

They encountered many other geysers along the way. Will told her there were about one hundred and fifty geysers visible in a distance of approximately one mile. Beehive Geyser, behind Old Faithful, had a narrow cone shape, which seemed to act as a nozzle for the eruption. Plume Geyser was the closest to the walkway, and its eruption could be viewed close-up. Heart Spring resembled a human heart. Crossing over the Firehole River, they found Castle Geyser and also encountered Riverside Geyser, which erupted on a slant. There was so much to see from Saw Mill, whose eruptions looked like a rotating circular blade, to Beauty Pool, with its rainbow-colored bacteria. It seemed like a fantasy world with the mist drifting through the air. Will knew so much; Deborah felt fortunate to have him as her personal guide.

After leaving the parking lot, Will enjoyed showing Deborah the favorite places he had found while exploring the park on previous trips. They drove to West Thumb, turning toward Bridge Bay, located near Yellowstone Lake. Will parked the car and found a picnic table with a view of the water. Deborah took the picnic basket, borrowed from the resort, and began removing their lunch.

They talked about their children, and the hurdles they would have explaining their feelings for each other. Will confessed his depression had been due to his son and daughter-in-law separating. The close attachment to his son was very evident. He mentioned his daughter needing her independence but didn't discuss the rebellious streak she had or how possessive of him she had become since her mother's death.

Deborah shared her children's feelings of not wanting another father. They had gotten used to her solitary life, and they might be shocked to know she was spending time with Will.

They decided not to tell their families about the reunion until they were certain their relationship would survive.

When they left Bridge Bay, the sun was beginning to set; they took the long way around the lower loop, passing Fishing Bridge and Canyon Village. It had been an enchanting trip to the most unusual place Deborah had ever visited.

Returning to the resort, Will mentioned how Big Sky became a popular vacation spot in the 1970s, not long before they went their separate ways.

"It will always be the special place God chose to bring us together," Deborah proclaimed.

"Tomorrow, we'll go horseback riding. There's a waterfall I want to show you."

Will began to yawn as they pulled into the parking area. "It's been a long day; we'll need to leave early."

"It's been an exceptional day. You meant everything to me once. To have a second chance seems impossible."

"Deborah, with God all things are possible."

Deborah agreed with Will; it was time to say good night. She had phone calls to make and some notes to record concerning Yellowstone and Big Sky. Will mentioned some facts not found while doing her research. Deborah promised to put her laptop away, but she had signed a contract, and the first draft couldn't be delayed.

At Deborah's door, Will kissed her sweetly on the lips, and then touched her gently on the nose. He walked down the hall toward his room as Deborah stood watching. Looking back he winked and gave her an affectionate two-fingered salute.

Deborah went inside wanting to contact everyone she knew, to tell them how happy she felt. She knew, of course, she would have to wait to tell Megan and her sons. There was one family member who would keep a confidence, Deborah thought. She couldn't resist and called her sister.

"Hi, Nancy."

"Deborah, why are you calling? What's wrong?"

"Nothing, everything is fantastic. You sound sleepy."

"Well, it's late here in Virginia."

"I'm sorry."

"What is it, Deborah?"

"Nancy, you will never believe what happened. I met a man."

"Oh, you did?"

"Well, not just any man. I met Will, or as we called him, Billy Dougherty."

"No! Is he there with his wife?"

"He's a widower."

"How interesting, tell me more."

"It's a long, involved story, but we said we wouldn't tell our children. I just had to tell someone. We seemed to have picked up from where we left off years ago."

"Just be careful not to rush into anything. You know how devastated you were the last time you broke up."

"We've agreed to take our time. We believe God brought us together. I'm sorry I woke you. I forgot about the time difference."

"Please keep me informed. I want to know all of the details."

Deborah felt relieved to share with her sister, if just for a short time, what God was doing. She tossed and turned, but grinned at the thought of her "old" friend. It was almost unbelievable to have Billy in her life again.

Chapter Eight

Will called the next morning to ensure Deborah hadn't slept in. She answered him saying she had been up for hours, and offered to make breakfast before their ride up the mountain.

As Deborah put the coffee on, Will knocked at the door. He looked rested, and she envied his having a full night's sleep. She didn't share with him the call to Nancy or the fact she didn't rest well. It was then Will teased, "Your eyes look a little droopy this morning. Have trouble sleeping?"

She gave him a frown of disapproval, then grinned from ear to ear. She knew he was just kidding.

"Everything smells delicious. I'm hungry."

"The food's almost ready. Remind me to take my cell phone with me. The children could call, and they worry if I don't answer."

"You're in good hands."

Deborah grasped Will's hands. "And such big strong hands, although my children aren't aware of you being here."

Deborah dropped his hands and put the eggs and toast on the table. "Would you like your coffee with cream or sugar?"

"I take my coffee black, or hadn't you noticed?"

"You didn't drink coffee in school. There's so much to learn about each other. We've definitely been affected by the separate lives we've led," she added.

"It will take time, but I'm willing to invest it—to explore the reason we met by chance."

"It wasn't by chance. I thought we agreed it was God's plan."

"Chance was a poor choice of words. You know I feel God's hand is guiding us. It's a long trip up the mountain. We'd better leave."

Deborah collected the dishes and loaded them into the dishwasher. "I'm ready! Lead on cowboy."

"I haven't asked you: Do you know how to ride?"

"Of course. My grandparents had a farm; I rode when we'd visit them. I'm sure I told you about it. Grandfather was an excellent horseman; he taught all of his children and grandchildren to ride."

"The trail can be rough. It's good to know you have experience."

As they reached the stables, Deborah saw the winding trail up the mountain. "How long do you think it should take?"

"About two or three hours; we won't go to the top. There's a trail near my favorite waterfall. It's where we'll start our descent."

"Sounds great, let's go."

Will knew the owner of the stable, so he asked if they could make the trip without a guide. Normally, he only permitted his employees to take the horses. He knew how experienced Will was, as he had ridden with him on numerous occasions, so he agreed to allow them to ride unescorted. With bears and other wildlife roaming freely, they needed to be prepared for any unforeseen encounter, so he insisted Will take a rifle for their safety. Will went back to the car and pulled his gun from the trunk.

Deborah was surprised. "Do you always carry a weapon in your car?"

"I keep it and extra fishing gear in a storage unit near the resort. It makes it easier to transport. Of course, the airline won't let me have a rifle on the plane."

After choosing the horses and having them saddled, they made their way up the trail. It was well worn, and Deborah knew many people had taken the path, including Will's wife. She couldn't help but wonder if the places she and Will had been visiting were reminders of Sherry.

Will looked like a real cowboy atop his horse. Deborah couldn't believe the city boy could be so comfortable in the saddle. "Will, I can't remember you ever riding horses in Pittsburgh. When did you start riding?"

"Sherry's family had horses; she taught me."

Deborah was sorry she had asked the question. There was a tightening in the pit of her stomach. How could she know she was the one Will wanted to be with? Deborah felt horseback riding was just another reminder of his wife.

They rode up the trail without speaking. Will broke the silence by whispering, "Look, over on the ridge." A doe and her fawn were eating. They seemed so peaceful. "We have about five minutes before we reach the waterfall. We'll dismount and rest before making our descent."

As they approached the waterfall, Will jumped from his horse and helped Deborah down. Taking the reins, Will tied them to a tree while Deborah walked to the cliff's edge to get a better look. Will stepped behind her and cradled her neck in his arms. He kissed the back of her hair gently and said, "This is the prettiest place I've found in my travels." Deborah took in the view and couldn't recall anything to match it. There was a rainbow reflected in the rising mist of the waterfall, a glorious confirmation of God's presence. Then she felt her stomach tighten again.

"Will, tell me the truth. Are you thinking about Sherry?"

"I would be lying if I said she hadn't crossed my mind."

"Will, I can't do this."

"What do you mean?"

"Sharing the places you've been with your wife, the special places reminding you of Sherry."

Will spun her around to face him. "I know who I've brought with me today. There's no mistaking who you are. No, you're not Sherry, and yes, this was a special place. But I wanted to share it with *you*. God's beauty doesn't change with the people who view it. Trust me, Deborah; you're no substitute for Sherry."

"Let's start down now," said Deborah. She didn't know how to respond to Will's remarks.

Will held the reins as Deborah mounted her horse. He then lifted himself onto his saddle and led the way down the steep hillside. There was an awkward silence, but Deborah felt she needed time to trust his feelings.

A peaceful little stream appeared, and Deborah could hear the rippling of the water on the rocks. Will rode ahead.

As he entered the water, his horse was startled and bolted, tossing Will to the ground. Deborah sprung from her horse, and ran to him. It was then she noticed a snake swimming downstream. "Will, are you okay?" He didn't answer. "Will,"

Deborah yelled. He didn't move. Deborah ran back to her horse. Retrieving the cell phone from her pack, she frantically called 911. The male dispatcher informed her that help would be sent immediately but he needed to know their location. Deborah looked around; the area was unfamiliar territory to her. She yelled out, "Will, wake up." Will's eyes opened slightly. "Will, where are we? What is this place called?" He answered in a muffled voice, "Below Bear Falls at Sutter's Stream." Deborah relayed the message as Will lost consciousness again.

"Lord, help me," Deborah cried. "Will, don't die. Please don't die." Deborah dropped the phone, placing her hands on Will's bruised head, as she began to pray. "Jesus, help us and heal Will of these injuries." Will opened his eyes again, looking up at her. "Debby, I love you," he moaned as he passed out. What had he said? It was the first time he had called her Debby in a very long time. She lowered her head to kiss him and then reached for her phone.

She had programmed Rev. Benning's number into the directory, so she pressed the call button. Robert was shocked to hear the news and said he and Susan would pray immediately. He asked Deborah if there was a hospital in the area. Deborah knew of only one, Bozeman. She told Robert she would let him know if Will would be taken there.

It seemed like an hour, but it was only twenty minutes before three paramedics arrived on four-wheelers, one pulling a flat trailer. The slope to the stream was too steep for the trailer, so two of the men grabbed a cloth stretcher, and without delay, descended the hill. They checked Will's vital signs and placed him on the stretcher. One of the men yelled,

"Joey, call for a helicopter transport to the clearing above us, the hillside is too steep for us to carry him to the trailer." Deborah saw the man on the top of the hill signal he heard them. The two others fastened straps around Will.

"Tie the horses to a nearby tree, Joey will take them back and follow us," one paramedic told Deborah. "The helicopter will be waiting. Oh, bring that rifle; we may need it."

Deborah obeyed his orders, tying the horses and pulling the rifle from the saddle. The paramedics carried Will over the stream and up a narrow path. In a few minutes, Deborah could hear the whirring noise of the helicopter as it flew above them. They came to a clearing just as the chopper touched down. The men hurried to put Will onboard and instructed Deborah to sit in front. Will was pale, and from the look on their worried faces, the men were anxious to lift off.

Will went in and out of consciousness several times. He seemed to be aware of his situation, but he continued to pass out. Deborah was concerned he wasn't moving. She called Rev. Benning to inform him they were on their way to Bozeman.

The helicopter arrived at the hospital within minutes. The physician on duty spent a long time assessing Will's condition. The doctor emerged through the double doors leading to the examining rooms and informed Deborah of Will's apparent paralysis. The doctor explained the need to move Will to another facility soon, as the hospital was not equipped to deal with his limitations.

Paralysis! The word stuck in her mind. How would Will take the news, she wondered. Just then, Robert and Susan walked through the emergency room door.

"How is Will?" Robert was anxious to know his condition.

"The doctor said he's been paralyzed; he'll need to be treated at another hospital. He'll remain here until he's stable."

Since he was clergy, Robert went to the admission desk, requesting permission to pray for Will, and a nurse opened the doors, allowing him to enter the treatment area. Deborah and Susan went to the waiting room where Susan consoled Deborah by telling her, "God will see you through this tragedy."

"Oh Susan, I was so insecure. I challenged Will about my role in his life. I thought he was taking me to places that reminded him of Sherry. I was being too emotional about the past, and I didn't want to trust his feelings. I know now, he does love me. He told me the first time he regained consciousness. I feel Will's accident was my fault. He was angry with me when he started down the hillside. Maybe he would have paid attention and not fallen from his horse. How will he accept the extent of his injuries?"

"You're not to blame, what happened was unfortunate but unpredictable. The important thing to believe is that Will is going to come out of this—God will sustain him. It may only be temporary. We've been praying for God's healing power to touch him. With God all things are possible."

"Will just quoted the same scripture to describe our relationship. I suppose I didn't realize how much I loved Will. God must have brought us together, He has given us a second chance."

Robert appeared, but the look on his face was daunting. It didn't reflect the composure she wanted to see.

"Robert, how is he?" asked Susan.

"Not well; we need God to intervene."

Streams of tears flowed as Deborah finally released the pent-up stress of the situation. Susan held her, trying to calm her by repeating, "Deborah, he'll be fine. We need to trust God."

Chapter Nine

When Will awoke, he was aware of his surroundings, but the doctor conveyed to Deborah the seriousness of his condition. He had severe bruising and had no feeling from the waist down. Deborah didn't want her feeling of hopelessness to show, but Will saw through her facade. "Deborah, I can deal with this. I need to know if you can."

"Will, I love you. I will be here for you as long as you need me."

"I've asked the doctors if I can be moved to a hospital in Atlanta. Robert called my children, and they're extremely worried. I need them with me."

"I can cancel my room and go with you."

"No, Deborah, you should return home or stay on here."

"What are you saying? I want to be near you, too. Didn't you say you loved me?"

"Yes, but the circumstances are different now. It's too much to ask of you. It's not fair for you to change your plans and put your life on hold. Your family will be waiting for you to return."

"Fair! You talk about fair. Why do you want to put the distance between us? How can God be so cruel as to reunite us, only to make you go through this suffering? And now you want me to leave?"

"I'm glad to know you really care, but don't blame God. Whatever we go through is for His purpose, and we'll understand some day why this has happened."

"Forgive me, Will. It's just . . . my heart is breaking for you. I didn't mean to blame God. What can I do?"

"We're going to accept God's will, and I'll return to Atlanta."

"Not without me you don't. I'll speak with Susan and Robert to see if I can stay with them and then I'll notify my children so they don't worry."

"If you insist, that should work. I'm too weak to challenge you. You always had to have things your way, if I recall correctly."

Deborah felt guilty for her attitude, knowing the pain Will was suffering. Bending to touch Will's cheek she whispered, "You may never be rid of me." Will struggled to kiss Deborah on the forehead, but she raised her chin, kissing him softly on the lips.

The anxiety she felt over his accident hindered any further research on her novel, so she relocated to a hotel near the hospital. Deborah was told Will would be going through testing so she pulled out the laptop and tried to write.

Alan doubted his ability to try out for the Olympics. Beverly wanted to encour—

That isn't what I want to say.

The Olympics seemed out of reach to Alan, and Beverly knew he was discour—

Deborah stared at her screen before shutting her laptop in frustration. *Why can't I concentrate? I'll never get this done, so I might as well give up.* Any attempt to work on her novel seemed futile; Deborah couldn't make sense of the words she wrote.

She spent a few sleepless nights praying for Will's recovery, and every moment the hospital would allow, she was at his side. When he was awake, he saw the dark circles under her eyes and begged her to rest, but she was too worried about his welfare to be concerned about her own.

Will was being sedated, and he slept most of the day. Deborah was satisfied just to be near him. She would put her head on the side of Will's bed and whisper to him. She would reassure him that she was with him forever. "You don't have to worry about my love; there is nothing that will keep us apart, not now, not ever." Deborah often fell asleep in the chair until the staff would ask her to leave.

After showing progress, the doctors made arrangements to transport Will to a hospital in Atlanta. Fortunately, Deborah's flight was routed through Atlanta, and she succeeded in exchanging her original ticket for one returning the same day as Will. Deborah was booked early the next morning for a flight to Hartsfield-Jackson Airport.

Susan and Robert had returned home a day earlier and called Deborah to inform her they would be at the airport to meet her. They also offered to take her luggage home with them when they dropped her off at the hospital. Deborah felt blessed to have friends like the Bennings.

She was anxious to see Will, though a little apprehensive about meeting his family. Will was a good man and seemed to have made a wonderful life for himself. Now she was faced with having to see if she could really fit into another family. His family.

Chapter Ten

Walking through the door of his hospital room, Deborah greeted Will with a smile. He looked rather pale and was still terribly bruised from his fall.

"How was your flight, Will?"

"Great, and how was yours?"

"I didn't like flying alone."

"What do you mean? Wasn't the flight full?"

"Oh, there were plenty of passengers, but you weren't with me. I was worried about you the entire trip and anxious to know how you were doing during your transport."

"They had paramedics onboard to make me comfortable."

Deborah reached for Will's hand. As they spoke, Will's daughter entered the room. "Katie, it's good to see you."

"Daddy, how are you?" Will's daughter noticed Deborah slip her hand from his. Katie gave her a disapproving glance.

"Katie, this is Deborah Miller. She was with me when I fell from the horse."

"Daddy, how could you fall? You're a good horseman."

"A snake spooked the horse, and I was thrown to the ground. It was fortunate that Deborah was there to call for help and take care of me until the paramedics arrived."

"Oh Daddy, I was really worried. I'm glad they brought you home so we can take care of you." Katie didn't want to acknowledge the woman who had been holding her father's hand.

"Katie, you shouldn't be rude. I just introduced you to Mrs. Miller."

"I'm sorry. It's good to meet you. Are you from Atlanta?" Katie wasn't interested in being polite to Deborah and only spoke to appease her father.

Recognizing the coldness in Katie's question, Deborah replied, "I'm from New Jersey; I'll be staying in town with Susan and Robert Benning." Deborah could feel the opposition from Will's daughter but didn't want to do anything to create additional animosity.

Feeling uncomfortable, Deborah turned and said good-bye to Will, then left the room. His family would see to his needs for the night, so she stopped at the nurses' station to get the number for a taxi. The tension from meeting Katie just added to her exhaustion. She needed rest and was also anxious to speak with her children.

ℱ

Katie was relieved to see Deborah go. She wondered who she was, why she had been with her father during the accident, and why she would be holding his hand. Before she could question her father about this strange woman, her brother Todd entered the room.

"Dad, how are you doing? We were shocked to hear the news."

"I'll be fine, son. The doctors feel the paralysis is only temporary, and the bruises will heal."

Todd knew his father was just trying to make light of the situation. He loved that about his dad. When there was a crisis, he could always count on his dad to make things seem better than they really were.

Todd had been feeling guilty about his father's trip to Big Sky. Will had made the decision shortly after Todd told him that he was separating from his wife and that Will's grandsons would be moving to Colorado with their mother. He felt his father was escaping Atlanta so he wouldn't be at home when they left.

Todd's family had moved in with Will after Sherry died. They were a great comfort to him, and he adored Todd's wife, Jamie. It was a very difficult time for Will when he heard they would be leaving. "Todd, you just missed meeting Daddy's friend," Katie said sarcastically. "She was with Dad when he had his accident. She's staying with Rev. Benning."

"I didn't know anyone was with you, Dad. I'm glad to know you weren't alone."

"Deborah Miller is the woman's name, Katherine. She was able to call for help, and I appreciate her coming to Atlanta. I would also appreciate you both being courteous to her while she's here."

Todd raised his eyebrows at Will's remarks. His father only called his sister Katherine when he was upset with her. He seemed to sense from something in his father's tone that Mrs. Miller wasn't just any woman horseback riding with him. Todd was intrigued at the prospect of getting to speak with her. "I look forward to meeting the woman who saved Dad's life."

"You'll have to forgive me now. I'm tired and should probably rest," said Will.

"We'll see you tomorrow, Daddy," said Katie.

As they walked into the hallway, Katie grabbed Todd by the arm and scolded him for his apparent interest in Deborah. She recounted how Deborah had been holding Will's hand when she walked into the room. She thought it was inappropriate for a strange woman to be visiting with their father, and especially to be holding his hand.

"Katie, how can you feel that way about someone you don't even know? She was there to help Dad, and we should be grateful."

"I'm not going to be grateful; I think she has an ulterior motive. Aren't you a little curious why they were together?"

"Dad is a grown man, and we don't dictate who he spends his time with or where he can go."

"Someone should be concerned about his choices."

"You have always been suspicious of everything, Katie, and frankly I don't agree with you. Dad's recovery should be our first concern. I'm sure if there is anything going on between him and Mrs. Miller, we will be told eventually." Todd did have a curiosity about the situation, but he felt his sister was being overly protective of their father.

Chapter Eleven

When Deborah arrived at the Bennings', Susan and Robert wanted to know about Will and asked, "Did everything go well with Will's trip from Montana?"

"Yes, he was exhausted from the flight but was in a good mood. I think he was relieved that his children wouldn't have to worry about his condition but could visit with him."

"Were the children at the hospital?" Susan was curious if they would accept Deborah.

"Not when I first arrived, but Katie came shortly after, and our introduction was quite awkward. She saw me holding Will's hand and gave me a look of disapproval. It's understandable the trepidation Will's daughter would have at seeing a stranger with her father, but I wanted to make a good first impression." Deborah wondered how her own children would have reacted. She knew she'd better call them before going to bed.

"You must be worn out with the day you've had," Susan said. "I'll show you to the guest room so you can unwind."

Deborah thanked Susan for allowing her to stay with them. She was glad the Bennings had been at Big Sky to help her through the ordeal of Will's trauma. When Susan left the room, Deborah took the cell phone from her purse and called her daughter. "Megan, I'm in Atlanta and staying with the Bennings; I just wanted to keep you informed."

"Mom, I don't understand. Why did you go to Atlanta? Your reservations were for a week in Montana."

"Megan, I was horseback riding with someone I met at the resort. He's a friend of Susan and Robert Benning. There was an accident, and they airlifted him to a hospital near his home in Atlanta."

"Why did you have to go with him?"

"Megan, it's a long story, and I'm tired from the flight and getting settled with the Bennings. Please understand I need to be here right now."

"I'm still not sure why it's important for you to stay there. Call me tomorrow."

"Good night, and kiss the children for me. I love you."

Deborah touched the *end call* button on her phone. She wished she could have told Megan about Will, but it was just too soon. She would wait until the next day to call Neal and Ryan. Her sons wouldn't be as curious about her change of plans. Deborah thought she'd better contact her sister. She knew Megan would probably call her to see if she knew anything about the situation.

"Hello, Nancy."

"Hi, Deborah, where are you?"

"I'm in Atlanta. I'm staying with Susan and Robert Benning."

"What's happening?"

"Will has been paralyzed from being thrown from a horse. He's pale and bruised, but his spirit is remarkable."

"What are they doing for his condition?"

"He's being treated for pain, but we've been told there should be signs of improvement soon if the paralysis is temporary."

"How are you feeling?"

"I'm exhausted but want to be here until he improves."

"Doesn't he have family in Atlanta who can care for him?"

"Yes, his children are here. I met his daughter today."

"How did that go?"

"It didn't go very well. She walked into the room while Will was holding my hand, and she was very cold toward me. I'm hoping to meet his son tomorrow. Maybe it will go better. I just had to let you know the facts. I haven't told my children about Will, and Megan may call you for more information. She only knows there was an accident and I'm staying with the Bennings. I would appreciate your confidence until I can tell my kids the entire story."

"I'm here for you, Sis. Whatever you need, just keep me informed. We'll be praying for Billy's recovery."

"Thank you, Nancy. I'd better get some rest. It's been a very long day."

"Good night, Deb."

Deborah thought of Katie's reaction to her being in Will's room. It might be difficult to change his daughter's first impression of her. She wondered if his son would be more accepting. She hoped her presence in Atlanta wouldn't create problems for Will. She was just too tired to worry about it and whispered a prayer for the Lord to take care of the situation.

Chapter Twelve

Todd arrived at the hospital early. He wanted to satisfy his curiosity about the woman his dad met at Big Sky.

Will was sitting in a wheelchair reading the newspaper when Todd walked into the room.

"How are you this morning, Dad? I see you're reading the *AJC*?"

"I'm feeling much better, just catching up with the local news. The soreness from my bruises seems to be leaving. I just wish I didn't have to sit in this wheelchair."

"You'll be fine. I spoke with the doctor yesterday, and he said the paralysis will only be temporary."

"What brings you in this early? You usually sleep past eight o'clock."

"I was anxious to see you. I called Jamie last night and told her about your accident. She was really worried, but I told her you'd be up in no time. Jamie said she will bring the twins to see you next week."

"I'm glad to hear that. I miss them when they're not around," Will said.

"I miss them all. She and I have been talking about our difficulties, and we're going to try to work through them. Their visit will allow me time to try and resolve some of our issues."

"You shouldn't work as hard as you do. We can afford to employ additional help. Life is too short to lose those we love. Not being there to enjoy the important events in their lives just isn't worth it. Your mother and I had a unique relationship. We worked together, so we spent most of our time with each other. You wanted to help with the business, so you were always a part of our world. We didn't have the quality time with your sister, and I think it was the reason for her rebellion."

Todd interrupted, "Not to change the subject, but Katie was pretty upset about the woman with you yesterday. She seems to be concerned that Mrs. Miller may have feelings for you."

"Son, Deborah Miller was a real godsend. It wouldn't have been much of a vacation without her. I met her the first day at the resort. Having her with me when I was thrown from the horse was a blessing. She's a friend of the Bennings."

"How does she know Rev. Benning?" Todd questioned.

"Deborah's brother attended Bible College with Robert Benning. It was a real surprise when we met him in town. I had taken Deborah to buy groceries, and I was shocked when he recognized her. Robert invited us to their cabin for dinner, and we spent the evening with the Bennings . . . but," Will sighed, "there's much more to the story."

"You can tell me, Dad. I'm anxious to hear what happened."

"Todd, I can't tell Katie right now. You have to promise to keep this confidential."

Todd's curiosity heightened. "Okay, Dad."

"Deborah and I met years ago. In fact, we went to school together. She was my first love and best friend during that time. We went our separate ways after high school and never saw each other until this week in Montana. Deborah's husband died several years ago, and she had gone to Big Sky to write."

"Did you know her immediately?"

"She has changed physically, and of course, we are both older, so I never associated the likeness to someone I knew over thirty years ago. When Robert called her by her maiden name, I realized who she was."

Todd was eager to know more. "How did Robert recognize her?"

"Deborah had seen the Bennings at her brother's new church dedication last year. It was the coincidental meeting of Robert that revealed her identity."

"You were born in Pittsburgh; does Deborah live there?"

"Deborah lives in New Jersey near her children. She insisted on being here until my condition improved. I'd like her to stay at our house, but Katie wouldn't understand. Susan and Robert have made their home available, and it should work in the short term. Todd, this may sound strange coming from your father, but I love Deborah more than I thought I could love another woman. I loved your mother, and we had a very rare bond. I'll never forget the wonderful life we had and how precious she was to me. But now God has blessed me with the exceptional woman I cared for long ago."

"Does Deborah feel the same way?"

"Yes, but I haven't asked her to marry me yet. I want to wait until I know I can walk down the aisle. It's not my intention to let her get away this time."

Todd was astounded. "It's really serious then, isn't it?"

"Yes, I want you to know Deborah for the kind and loving person she is. I would like you to take her to our house; she should see the place I want her to live someday. I hope she will want to be married in the garden, but I want it to be her decision. Will you do that for me, Todd?"

"Sure, Dad, whatever you want. It does seem sudden, but I understand your feelings for Deborah. In fact, I'm really happy you've found someone to enjoy life with again. Though I'm not sure Katie will understand."

"I can't explain my feelings to Katie yet. I want her to appreciate Deborah before she hears about my plans."

"I'm glad you confided in me. I felt Deborah must be special to you. If you say God brought you together, he can work things out with Katie. I'm sure she will accept Deborah eventually."

"Katie's been very possessive; I hope I can keep her from hurting Deborah. I'll need to keep them from visiting at the same time until I know Katie won't make a scene."

Chapter Thirteen

The smell of coffee brewing woke Deborah. She looked at the clock and saw it was nine in the morning. Feeling guilty for sleeping late, she quickly showered, dressed, and went downstairs, where she found her hostess sitting at the kitchen table reading the morning newspaper.

"Good morning, Deborah. I hope you had a pleasant sleep."

"It was just what I needed. Now, I must hurry to the hospital before Katie visits Will."

"Oh, don't let Katie scare you. She's just been protective of her father since Sherry died. It's her way of coping with her mother's death."

"What do you mean?"

"Katie was a very independent teen and gave Sherry a difficult time. It was not your average mother/daughter relationship. Katie was very confrontational. Sherry tried everything to please her, but nothing seemed to work. When she graduated from college, she moved into her own apartment. Then Sherry got sick, and Katie wanted to move back home. Will refused to let her guilt ruin Sherry's final months. He wanted Sherry at peace for as long as possible. Although Will adores his daughter, he didn't want to complicate things for

Sherry at the end. Katie has been dealing with the guilt of how she treated her mother ever since."

"What about his son?"

"Todd was always an obedient boy. He was anxious to help his dad with the business, and he treasured his mother. He would say, 'No one has a better mom than me.' When Sherry died, Will insisted Todd and Jamie live with him."

"Will mentioned Todd and Jamie have separated."

"Yes, unfortunately. Jamie attended our church and told me how Todd had become obsessed with being successful and seemed to have drifted from her and the boys, spending less and less time with them. She doesn't really want a divorce, but taking the boys to stay with her parents was to give Todd time to decide what was most important to him. Will was hurt when he heard Jamie and the boys would be leaving. Will adores those boys. He felt somewhat at fault, giving Todd most of the responsibility for the business. In fact, it's the reason Will was at Big Sky. He said he needed a vacation, but I think he felt Todd and Jamie could work things out if they had the house to themselves. In a way, I think Will felt he could also find solace at Big Sky. Will and Sherry would go to Big Sky when problems became overwhelming. It was their hideaway. When they returned home, they could deal with the difficulties generated by the business and family."

"He did seem rather melancholy when I first saw him, but he didn't tell me how deeply he felt about the situation with Todd's family."

"That sounds like Will. His face shows his feelings but he keeps everything inside. Now we better get to the hospital."

"I'm not sure what I would have done without you and Robert during this time. I appreciate all you've done for me."

Susan stood up, "Nonsense, Deborah, we're just blessed to have you staying with us. We know Will can also rest easier knowing you're taken care of. I'll find Robert; he can come to the hospital with us."

The drive to the hospital took only minutes, but Deborah found herself anxiously desiring to see the man she loved.

Will and Todd were talking when Deborah, Susan, and Robert entered the room. Deborah was a little disappointed. She wanted to embrace Will, but she knew it wasn't possible with Todd present.

"Where's my hello kiss?" asked Will.

Deborah was surprised and turned to face Todd. He extended his hand saying, "Hello, Mrs. Miller, I'm Todd. Dad and I had a long talk before you came. I wouldn't want you to disappoint my father," Todd spoke while grinning at the woman his sister had called strange.

"It's very nice to meet you, Todd." Deborah turned back toward Will and leaned over to kiss him. "How are you feeling today?"

"Super! If only I had the use of my legs, everything would be perfect."

Todd saw a glow in his father's face; one he hadn't seen for a long time. "You seem to bring out the best in my dad. I approve of the TLC you've given him."

"Thank you, Todd. Your father mentioned how proud he was of you during our stay at Big Sky."

"Yes, what a coincidence for you both to be in Montana at the same time."

"Todd, I told you we feel it was part of God's plan for us," admonished Will.

"Of course, Dad; it's just unbelievable you could meet in Montana after all these years."

"With God, all things are possible," responded Will, smiling at Deborah.

"You're right. I need to have more faith," Todd admitted.

Robert Benning answered with a very loud "Amen."

Todd turned to look at the Bennings. "Susan, you and Rev. Benning should be seeing me in church. Dad and I have decided to change our Sunday hours."

"Terrific, Todd, we'll look forward to having you worship with us," said Susan.

Todd walked to Will's side. "Now, I have to go to work." Todd put his hand on Deborah's shoulder. "Take good care of my dad."

"I will, Todd."

"Anyone responsible for my dad feeling this well in a hospital bed has my approval."

Robert and Susan walked out with Todd. They wanted to get a cup of coffee and give Will and Deborah time alone.

Will reached for Deborah's hand. "Todd is going to take you to my house tonight. I want you to see how God has blessed me. Betsy, my housekeeper, will show you around."

"I'm looking forward to seeing your home."

"Hopefully, one day, it will be our home."

"When will you speak with Katie?"

"I told Todd I wanted to wait until she has a chance to get to know you."

"That might take a while. She wasn't very pleased to see us holding hands yesterday."

"She's always been stubborn but she'll come around."

"I hope so. It's my prayer to have all of our children happy for us."

"My children's acceptance is also my prayer; I feel Todd already is accepting of our relationship."

Robert and Susan returned and joined in the conversation. It was about noon when Robert told Deborah, "We will be leaving now, but give us a call when you need a ride back to our house."

Will spoke up. "Robert, Todd is coming about four o'clock to take Deborah to my house. Betsy will make dinner, so you and Susan will be free to take care of church business. I've told Todd to give Deborah one of our cars to use while she's here."

"I know you want Deborah to see your home, but we want you to know we love having Deborah with us, and she is no bother."

"Thank you both for being so accommodating. I'm relieved to know Deborah is able to stay in Atlanta."

"She is welcome to stay as long as she'd like," Susan answered.

"If it weren't for Katie, she could stay at my house."

"Don't worry. Just recuperate, and let us enjoy having Deborah visit for the time being," Robert said.

"Now, Susan and I should allow you some time together before Todd arrives. Is Katie coming in today?"

"Yes, I told her to come after work."

"I can see you've been skillfully planning your visitors," added Robert.

"At this time, it seems necessary."

As Robert and Susan left, Deborah pulled a chair to the side of Will's bed. "Will, it seems as if time is standing still. When I close my eyes, I can imagine that we are teens again and so much in love. What really happened to keep us from spending our lives together? I almost feel cheated we've been apart so many years. You meant everything to me."

"I suppose it just wasn't to be. God had other plans for our lives. He knows what's best. I'm glad God arranged for us to be reunited. I love you, Deborah."

They talked about the time they would spend together and before they knew it, Todd arrived.

"Hi Dad, I'm here to pick up my dinner date. Are you ready, Mrs. Miller?"

"Yes, but please call me Deborah. I'm looking forward to our evening."

"Maybe I should sign myself out of this hospital. Don't have too much fun without me. After all, I found her first."

Deborah kissed Will and promised to see him early the next day. Todd opened the door and waited for Deborah to walk through. He turned to Will and winked. "Dad, I'll show her a good time."

Chapter Fourteen

As they left the hospital, Todd led the way to his car and held the passenger door open.

"Your father taught you well."

Todd got in, and pulled out of the parking lot. "Tell me about yourself, Deborah. Dad filled me in on the past, but I would really like to know about your family. How many children do you have?"

"I have three children. Megan, my daughter, is the oldest. She is married and has three daughters: Sara, Kathleen, and Valerie. Neal and Ryan are my sons' names. They haven't married yet. They've been too busy climbing the corporate ladder. My husband died several years ago. I believe stress from the responsibility of his position caused his heart attack. I remind the boys constantly of their need to enjoy life and not to be eager to gain possessions in this world. They're young and have desires they want to satisfy. Fast cars, designer clothes, and fine homes seem to be their focus these days. They attend church, but I'm not sure they have the love and desire for the things of God they once had. I pray they gain wisdom, and understand what's really important." Deborah realized she was striking a chord with Todd.

"Dad told me you're a writer." Todd wanted to change the subject. The comments concerning her sons and their desires for material things made him uncomfortable.

"Yes, I started writing seriously when my husband died. It's something I enjoy immensely. It also allows time for my family and my commitment to God. I love the Lord, and I feel nothing should come before Him. Everything works much smoother when He's in charge."

"Where does my dad fit in?"

"Todd, I feel God brought us together. Your father has a deep devotion to the Lord, and I didn't think I would find a man who felt as I do. It seems strange, after all these years, we would reunite."

Todd became quiet and softly said, "Deborah, I've been like your sons. It's been important to me to succeed in business and in finances and to gain my father's praise. I was losing my family and my relationship with God. My wife will be coming back next week to visit with Dad, and I would like you to help me pray she'll stay. I've realized it's been my fault; our lives were taking separate roads. I desperately want her back and want to see my sons raised in a Christian home."

"Todd, how encouraging. I'll pray that God will bless your marriage and your life."

They turned off the main road to a treelined driveway. "Are they magnolia trees?"

"Yes, they were my mother's favorite."

"I've never seen so many in one place before."

At the end of the driveway appeared a grand home with large white columns. It was what she envisioned an exquisite southern mansion should look like.

"Todd, what a magnificent home you have."

"It was Dad's gift to Mother on their twentieth anniversary. Mother grew up on a farm in Dawsonville, Georgia. She would tell us stories of how she and her sisters would pretend to be the O'Haras from the novel *Gone with the Wind*. She would insist upon playing Scarlett; mother had long dark hair like yours. When dad became successful, he was able to give her the home of her dreams. He insisted the contractor have the shell done to show her on their anniversary. Dad knew not to choose the fixtures or cabinets; he left that job for Mom. Mother was completely shocked when Dad handed her the keys. It took them about a year to finish the inside.

"For their twenty-fifth anniversary they had a costume barbeque. Mom dressed in a green gown, and Dad wore a tux. She called him Rhett, and of course, she got to play Scarlett again. They were so happy, but it was strange to see them dressed that way. Mom wore her hair in long curls and looked young and beautiful. Shortly after the party, she was diagnosed with cancer, and a few months later, she became bedridden. The memories of the barbeque meant a great deal to her. Dad bought her every *Gone with the Wind* collectible he could find. He purchased a large curio cabinet and put it in the bedroom for her to enjoy. Mother left her collectibles to my sister, but Katie admitted to Jamie that she would feel uncomfortable taking them out of the house." Todd hesitated, and then said, "I'm sorry to run on like this; I miss Mother, and it's difficult not to talk about her."

"It's important to remember the good times and special feelings you had for your mother."

As they pulled up to the house, the front door opened. "That's Betsy, our housekeeper. I think she's a little curious about you. She's been sworn to secrecy too." Todd leaped out of the car and opened Deborah's door.

A short, full-figured woman with reddish hair stood smiling in the open doorway.

"Hello, Todd," Betsy called out.

"Hello, Betsy, is dinner ready?"

"Almost; your father told me to have dinner at six thirty tonight."

"Betsy, this is Deborah Miller, Dad's friend."

"Hello, Deborah, I'm pleased to meet you. Mr. Dougherty wants me to show you around the house."

"Thank you, Betsy. It's nice to meet you. I'm looking forward to seeing the inside of Will's home. The outside is stunning."

Betsy and Todd showed Deborah through the house. It was like stepping into another era. Todd conveyed, "Mother insisted on decorating the house herself. The antiques were purchased from many parts of the country."

Each piece of furniture lovingly matched each room. The bedrooms were separated into two wings, with three bedrooms in each. Todd and his family slept in the west wing, and Will's room was in the east wing. Deborah noticed the large curio cabinet in a spare bedroom. Todd mentioned his father wanted it out of sight after his mother's death.

Betsy excused herself to finish dinner, and Todd took Deborah to the high porch overlooking the backyard. It was an impressive flower garden, with two large magnolia trees at the end of a long hedged walkway. Deborah thought it would make the perfect setting for a wedding. She imagined herself standing with Will between the magnolia trees.

Todd broke her train of thought by explaining how Will was responsible for planning the garden. "Dad has a gardener groom it once a week."

Will has really done well for himself, she thought. *What a fitting reward for his hard work.* "It's a pleasure to see your home. I knew your father when he had very little. He deserves the abundance God has given."

"I can remember some meager times in the beginning of his business, but I watched how Dad was blessed as he gave to the church. He never let work get in the way of his service to the Lord. I'm not sure when I got off track. I felt by working harder, I could accomplish much more. It was my way, not God's."

"It's important you've recognized that, Todd. It's never too late to make changes to create a better life for your family. Money isn't everything."

"Deborah, I can see why Dad loves you. You're a very special person. I'm glad you've come to Atlanta. Thank you for listening and sharing your thoughts with me tonight. It's been quite inspirational."

"Thank you, Todd. Now if only I can convince your sister. I would like to be her friend, which I know will be quite an accomplishment."

"Katie is pretty hardheaded, but she does need a friend. Mother's death was difficult for her. She had unresolved issues with Mother, and she tries to hide her grief. She's become extremely devoted to Dad. She and I have never been very close. Katie didn't accept anything I did or any of my friends. My wife tried to reach out to her, but Katie doesn't allow anyone to penetrate the wall she's built. She's a doting aunt to my boys though. She was upset to see them leave, and hadn't spoken to me until yesterday, at the hospital."

"I'll have to pray for God to open a door to reach Katie. It sounds like she really needs to accept love from others."

Betsy appeared in the doorway. "Dinner is ready."

"Thank you, Betsy."

Deborah and Todd walked into the mahogany-paneled dining room. An opulent crystal chandelier hung over the long table set for just the two of them.

"This is an exquisite room," remarked Deborah.

"It's a little big for my taste. It was always too formal. After the first year, Mother chose to have our meals served in the kitchen—except for special occasions."

"It would be splendid for large dinner parties, though I would have agreed with your mother. I believe in intimate family dinners. It's an opportunity for those we love to spend time together and share their day. I would suggest picking up our plates and moving, but Betsy has prepared the table beautifully for us; I wouldn't want to offend her."

"She wouldn't mind, although I know it was per Dad's instructions she sat us in here. He might be upset if we moved."

Betsy entered the dining room with a large platter heaped with pot roast, red potatoes, and carrots, and placed it in front of Deborah. The aroma of freshly baked bread drifted from the open door connected to the kitchen, and Betsy exited to get the yeast rolls she had just removed from the oven. When she returned Deborah commented, "Betsy, this looks and smells absolutely delicious."

"Thank you. I hope you enjoy it, but leave room for dessert. If you need anything else, I'll be in the kitchen."

When the little woman closed the door giving them privacy, Deborah asked, "How long has Betsy been part of your household?"

"Betsy was hired the first year my parents built the house. She has been a member of the family ever since. My children adore her. She was so attentive to Mother during her illness— caring for her and nursing her through some extremely rough times. She and Katie aren't very close though. Katie didn't live in the house very long and tends to treat Betsy as just hired help. Betsy was hurt by Katie's treatment of Mother before her cancer, and she would keep Katie away later when Mother was suffering."

"Betsy seems like an exceptional person. I'm looking forward to knowing her better."

Betsy appeared carrying an exquisitely decorated cake. "Would you like to have dessert now?"

"You must have a piece of Betsy's specialty."

"Betsy, you baked the cake?"

"Yes, I did."

"It's too pretty to eat."

"It tastes better than it looks. Betsy's cakes are the reason Dad and I have trouble with our waists. Betsy keeps us going to the gym."

"Then I must have a small slice."

After tasting the delicacy, Deborah sighed. "This is the best cake I've ever tasted."

Betsy beamed. "It was my momma's recipe, but I added some of my own ingredients."

"Where did you learn how to decorate cakes?"

"Actually, I've taught myself. I enjoy playing with the decorating tips and have made many cakes. I thought about taking a class or two, but Mr. Dougherty bought me some tapes about decorating, which have helped. Sorry, but I'm known to talk too much."

"You're extremely talented. Maybe you can show me how you do it."

"I would love to. Just let me know when you're ready."

"Dinner was delicious and dessert divine. I could be spoiled by such cuisine."

"Anytime you want to come for dinner, you're welcome. I'm sure it would be fine with Mr. Dougherty," said Betsy.

Deborah's cell phone began to ring. It was her son Neal. The frantic tone of his voice frightened Deborah. "Neal, what is it? I can't understand what you're saying."

"Mom, you have to come home. Ryan is in the hospital. He's had a terrible accident."

"What happened, Neal?"

"He was having dinner with a friend, and on the way home, he was hit by a truck. Mom, he's in critical condition. They took him to Camden Trauma Center. Hurry home, please."

"I'll be there as soon as I can book a flight." Deborah pushed *end call* and immediately phoned the Bennings. "Susan, I need your help."

From the urgency in her voice, Susan knew something was wrong. "What can I do, Deborah?"

"Please, get my suitcase and pack my things? I need to return home tonight. My son Ryan had a car accident. He's in critical condition, and I need to return immediately."

"My dear, I'll be glad to do that for you. I'll tell Robert; he can help us pray."

Deborah asked Todd if he would find the airline number for her and take her to the airport.

"Deborah, I'm very sorry to hear your sad news. Of course I'll help you."

After making the arrangements, Todd and Deborah got into his car and started toward the Bennings' home to pick up her bags. "Todd, will you stop by the hospital so I can tell your father about Ryan? I want to tell him in person."

"I think that's a good idea."

Arriving at the hospital, Deborah hurried to Will's room. She pushed the door open and ran to Will's side, tears rolling down her cheeks. "Oh Will, I have to return home immediately."

"What's wrong, darling?"

"Ryan has been hospitalized after having a car accident. Neal said he's critical, and it's imperative for me to return."

"I understand. How are you getting there?"

"Todd is waiting downstairs for me. I'll pick up my bags at the Bennings' and go straight to the airport. There is a flight leaving in three hours. I just wanted to tell you in person."

"Don't worry about me dear. Your family needs you. I love you, and I will pray for God to take care of your son."

She kissed him, and turned to rush out. It was then she saw Katie sitting in the corner of Will's room. Katie's eyes met Deborah's in an ice-cold stare. Deborah couldn't take the time to explain. She would have to let Will handle the situation. She hurried out of the hospital and into Todd's car.

They picked up her bags at the Bennings' home and made their way through Atlanta to the airport. Todd recognized the anxiety Deborah was going through, and he tried to calm her. He asked Deborah if she would like him to pray with her. Deborah agreed, and after prayer she felt a real peace about Ryan. She thanked Todd for his thoughtfulness and reassured him she would be fine.

Before going through security, Deborah hugged Todd and told him she would return to Atlanta when she could. Deborah thought what a blessing it was to have Todd there when she needed help.

<p>

Katie stood speechless, staring mercilessly at her father. What she had just witnessed was a definite shock to her system. Will broke the silence. "Katie, this isn't the way we planned to tell you."

All Katie could do was glare at Will. Her facial expressions spoke volumes. She would look angry, shocked, and then very melancholy. Finally, she found the strength to speak. "Even Todd knew about Mrs. Miller; you kept this a secret from me. How long has this been going on? Were you vacationing together in Montana? I never thought you would shut me out. I always wondered if I really belonged in this family. Dad, you were the only one I could believe in. Was I ever wrong!"

"Katie, please trust me. I love you."

"Really? After what I just witnessed. Good-bye, Dad. There's nothing else to say."

Katie walked toward the door, shoved it open, and disappeared from Will's sight. She wondered why her father and brother would want to deceive her. Who was Deborah anyway? Whoever she was, Katie vowed never to accept this woman as part of her life.

As she walked through the hospital doors to the outside, Katie felt the need to break all ties with her father and brother. She stopped by the nearest Target and bought boxes and bubble wrap. She was doing the only thing she knew would show her separation from the family. Katie drove to her father's home and rang the doorbell repeatedly. Betsy opened the door, and Katie thrust her way through, carrying the packing materials. She walked upstairs to the spare room and began wrapping the "treasures" her mother left to her.

Betsy frantically called Todd on his cell phone, and informed him about Katie's actions. He told her he had just turned onto Route 400 and would be home soon. "Hurry, Todd. I'm worried about Katie; she isn't acting right."

Todd returned home as Katie was packing the last box into her car. "What are you doing here, Katie?"

"Why shouldn't I be allowed in my parents' home?"

"That's not what I mean. You have scared Betsy."

"I'm taking what belongs to me, and I'm leaving for good."

"What are you talking about?"

"You and Dad are content to keep me in the dark about things, so you can just go on without me being in the way."

"Katie, you've always been stubborn, but this is ridiculous. Dad didn't keep you in the dark."

"You knew about Deborah. Why hadn't I ever heard her name before?"

"I didn't know about her until yesterday; don't be so unreasonable."

"When you see Dad, tell him I took my inheritance."

Katie got into her car and slammed the door. She squealed her tires on the way down the driveway. Todd stood in disbelief at the reaction his sister had to the revelation of Deborah.

Will's emotions were torn. He was confined to the hospital and couldn't follow his daughter to console her. Will was concerned he may lose her due to his affection for Deborah. He was also anxious for Deborah and the seriousness of her son's condition. He couldn't be much comfort to the women he loved. Will knew the only answer for both situations was prayer.

Chapter Fifteen

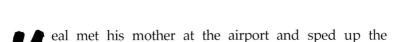

Neal met his mother at the airport and sped up the highway to the Camden Trauma Center.

"How is Ryan?"

"Mom, he is not doing well; the doctors told me the next twenty-four hours are critical. He had emergency surgery for internal bleeding after I spoke to you. He looks like a mummy; he has so many broken bones."

"What caused the accident? Who was he having dinner with?"

"His college roommate, Jonathan, came to Trenton for business, and they met at a restaurant for dinner. Ryan drove out of the parking lot and onto the interstate when a truck driver came across the median strip and hit him head on. Jonathan was driving behind Ryan and witnessed the accident. He immediately called for help. It was Jonathan who pulled Ryan from the car; he was afraid it might explode. He called me as soon as the ambulance came and explained the seriousness of Ryan's condition. I went directly to the hospital, but they wouldn't let me see him. That's when I called you."

"Who is with Ryan now?"

"Jonathan and Megan were at the hospital when I left."

"I'm thankful Jonathan was there and took action to get him help. What happened to the truck driver?"

"He was fine, just a few minor cuts. He is completely regretful and has taken full responsibility. I'm just glad he wasn't going fast."

Neal pulled to the front of the hospital, and told Deborah he would meet her in the intensive care unit after he parked his car.

As Deborah entered Ryan's room, Megan and Jonathan greeted her with distressing news: Ryan had lapsed into a coma. Deborah went to his side and quietly prayed. He looked helpless with an IV and multiple tubes connected to his seemingly lifeless body. She thought of her conversation with Todd concerning her sons and their ambitions. She closed her eyes and prayed for God to spare Ryan's life.

Jonathan had meetings he needed to attend the next day, so he hugged Deborah and said he would be calling later to check on Ryan's condition. It was close to daybreak when Megan left; she told her mother that she would return when her girls were on the school bus. Deborah couldn't bear to leave her oldest son, so she had Neal take her bags home and spent the night in the hospital. She wanted to be near Ryan if he regained consciousness.

As dawn came, Deborah went outside to view the sunrise. She reflected on all she'd been through during the week. *Life is fleeting*, she thought. *We never know what to expect. It is important to be prepared for any unforeseen event.* She stretched and thought of Will in Atlanta. She wondered how he handled the situation with Katie. Deborah regretted having to leave the way she did, and she couldn't get the look on Katie's face out of her mind.

Their first meeting had gone so wrong, and it was only made worse by the scene of Deborah's departure from the hospital the night before.

Thinking a cup of coffee would really be welcome after the night she'd just been through, Deborah walked inside to find the cafeteria. She sat sipping her coffee, trying to find some peace about Ryan and the possibility of complications should he survive. *He just has to survive.* Ryan was young and strong; he had everything to live for. Deborah promised herself she would accept whatever God felt was necessary to deal with Ryan (and Neal).

The accident affected Neal inwardly; Deborah knew she'd have to find time to comfort him. Telling Neal and Megan about Will would have to wait until Ryan was conscious. Deborah would delay explaining Will to them for several days, although she knew there would be questions about Atlanta, especially from Megan.

After leaving the cafeteria, she went back to Ryan's room. There had been no change. It was really too soon, though she had faith God was able to touch him at any time. At nine that morning, she decided to call Will. He must be wondering why she hadn't called the night before, but it was late when she arrived at the hospital, and she hadn't wanted to disturb him in his condition.

The phone rang in Will's room, and he lifted the receiver. "Hello, Will."

"Deborah, it's so good to hear your voice. How is Ryan doing?"

"The prognosis isn't good. I didn't call last night because he had just lapsed into a coma when I arrived. Megan stayed with me until long after midnight. Will, he looks awful. It was a very bad accident, and he has multiple broken bones and internal injuries."

"Darling, I'm sorry to hear the news. We've all been praying for him. Susan and Robert called last night to see if I had heard anything."

"Will, what happened with Katie? I was shocked to see her, and the look on her face seemed to reflect the same."

"Katie will be fine." Will didn't want to explain Katie's departure from his room. He hoped the situation would reverse itself by the time Deborah returned to Atlanta. There was no reason to worry Deborah when she had Ryan to agonize about.

"I'm not sure when I can return. Ryan's condition is grave. It may take months for his injuries to heal, and then the process of rehabilitation will begin. Right now, it's just important he regain consciousness."

"I'll have plenty of family and friends to look after me. Don't worry about returning until your son is well. I waited years for you. I can wait a few extra months, or as long as it takes."

"It's all been overwhelming—finding you and the accidents happening. I know everything will work out for the best. It's just difficult seeing two of the men I love most in this world suffering."

"With God's help, we'll make it through. Now keep me informed, and get as much rest as you can. Ryan will need your help when he's ready for rehabilitation."

"You're right. I haven't told Megan or Neal about us yet. I wanted to wait to also tell Ryan. I long to be with you, Will, and I don't want anything to separate us again."

"That won't happen. You're a very significant part of my life, and nothing can change the feelings I have for you."

"I'll keep you informed of Ryan's progress and let you know if there is any change. Thank Susan and Robert for their prayers."

"I'll call and let them know. They care and want to do anything they can to help."

Deborah returned to Ryan's room after her phone call. His nurse was checking the monitors, and Deborah thought she looked familiar. "Hello, I'm Ryan's mother," she said.

"Yes, I know, I'm Donna Roberts. I graduated from high school with Ryan. It must have been a terrible accident. His injuries are extensive, but his vital signs seem to be improving."

"That's great news. We've had everyone praying for him."

"I called my father and had our church pray for him as well."

"Of course, your father pastors a church in town. Donna, I'm glad you're Ryan's nurse. He needs more than just medication right now; he needs a miracle."

Chapter Sixteen

"Y ou must not give up. I won't allow you to give up on your dreams. There is so much more for you to experience!"

Ryan's nurse seemed to be out of breath as she entered his room. "Is there something wrong?"

"No, Donna, I'm sorry. I must have been louder than I should have been. I often read passages from my manuscript to Ryan. Even though he can't respond, I like to hear what I've written."

"It sounded a little ominous, and I felt I needed to check. Would you like another ear to listen? I have a break soon."

"I would enjoy that very much." Deborah was happy for the opportunity to have someone she could speak with. It had been over a month of sitting and waiting for any response from Ryan, and Deborah's other children spent less and less time at the hospital. Megan's family kept her busy, and her visits were short. The conversations with her mother concentrated on Ryan's condition. Neal was faithful and visited every evening after work. He spent the majority of his time contemplating the needs Ryan might have in the future. It was his way of coping while looking at his lifeless brother. It was evident Neal was in denial about the severity of Ryan's condition. Deborah didn't want to complicate their lives further by telling them about Will. She knew Will understood, but Deborah didn't like to keep their love a secret from her family.

During the days that followed, Deborah and Donna formed a close bond. Donna even revealed the crush she had once had on Ryan. Deborah knew in her heart everything would work out, and she continued to write (and read) her book.

The Committee called and said one of the skiers has a broken leg and can't compete. They offered me a spot in the upcoming Olympics.

Deborah paused from reading aloud and began to type a few more words.

"Why would they be calling you? Mom, you are too old for the Olympics."

Deborah was engrossed in her novel and almost didn't hear her son speak. When she finally realized it was Ryan, she yelled, "Ryan, you're awake! Donna, hurry, come in here. He's awake."

Donna rushed in and checked the monitors as she spoke to him. "Ryan, do you know where you are?"

"No, is this a hospital?"

"Yes, you had a terrible accident." Donna smiled at Deborah and said, "I need to inform the doctor."

Deborah, now at Ryan's side, was thanking God for His blessings. Tears of joy streamed down her cheeks.

"Mom, are you okay?"

"I'm fine now. You have been in a coma for over a month. Do you remember the car accident?"

"No, I just know I can't move my body."

"You're not paralyzed. You have multiple broken bones, but they will heal. It's only by God's mercy and grace you even lived."

When the doctor arrived, he asked Deborah if she would like to contact her family while he examined Ryan. Deborah knew it was a polite way to ask her to leave the room, even though she was anxious to inform everyone.

Deborah went outside and called Megan and Neal. Neal said he would be leaving the office immediately to be with them. Megan had to wait for someone to watch the girls. They were both excited, and relieved, to hear Ryan was finally conscious. Deborah then called Will and rejoiced with him, and she asked him to tell the Bennings. It was truly a time to be thankful. Deborah waited for the doctor to exit the room, to give her his report.

"Mrs. Miller, Ryan is responding well. He doesn't seem to have any complications from the coma. We'll run some tests tomorrow. I just request you try to keep him quiet and calm."

Donna was fussing with the tubes and was quite attentive to Ryan when Deborah walked into the room.

"Mom, do you remember Donna?"

"Well, I hadn't when you were admitted, but we've become great friends ever since. She has been wonderful company and has given you great care."

Ryan smiled his approval.

Though he was out of the coma, Ryan had to undergo additional surgeries that kept him hospitalized for another three months. Ryan's condition improved daily: he was sitting up and feeding himself, and the doctors were pleased with his progress. Deborah knew the numerous prayers of family and friends had been responsible for the change. She noticed Donna was also a factor in Ryan's recovery. Her diligent care seemed to grow into something special. Ryan didn't seem to mind all of the extra attention Donna gave him, including time after her shift had ended.

One day, Deborah walked into Ryan's room and saw them holding hands. It was a welcome relief to see her son conscious and content; although, she was reminded of the look on Katie's face, the first time they met.

Deborah's thoughts went to Will. It was odd he hadn't mentioned Katie during their conversations. Will went for rehabilitation during the time Ryan was in a coma. He had gone through the gradual process of learning how to handle tasks without feeling to his lower extremities and then with adjustments to his treatment as sensation returned to his body. He informed Deborah that he expected his discharge in a few days.

Changes were also taking place in Will's life. Jamie had moved back to be with Todd, and Will was ecstatic to have his grandsons home.

Ryan spoke, breaking her train of thought. "Mom, the doctor said he wants to send me to a center for therapy. I'll be moved by next week if they can locate a room."

"Ryan, that's exciting."

Just then, Neal and Megan walked through the door.

"We have fantastic news for you. Ryan will be moved to a rehab center soon."

Everyone was delighted with the announcement. Neal said, "I've done some checking on beds, lifts, and other equipment you might use when you come home. I also promise to visit the center to learn from the therapists how I can assist you."

"Slow down, brother. I haven't left the building yet," Ryan said with a smile.

"He's been planning a long time for this day and so have I," admonished Deborah.

"I love you all and can't thank you enough for the time you've spent with me this summer. Especially you, Mom."

A tear ran down Deborah's cheek. "It is a blessing just to see you regaining your strength." Deborah thought it might be a good time to tell them about Will. "Now that you're all together, I have something I've needed to tell you. Because of Ryan's accident, I've avoided explaining to you what has been happening in my life. You know I diverted my trip from Montana to Atlanta. I've been thankful I haven't been questioned on my reason for leaving. The injured man was a very old and dear friend. We had gone to school together and had been in love. We are convinced God reunited us after all these years, and we are going to pursue His will for us. His name is Will Dougherty."

Megan asked, "Mom, what does that mean exactly?"

"We'll probably marry next spring if everything works out. We weren't sure what would happen when he was paralyzed during his fall."

Neal asked, "How is Will now?"

"He's been convalescing; the paralysis was only temporary. Will is to be released from his care center in a few days."

Ryan inquired, "Why have you been tied to my bedside? Didn't you want to be with him, in Atlanta?"

"You're my son, and Will wants me to be with you. He understands you've needed me."

"If I were separated from Donna and given the chance to see her, you better believe I would be gone in a flash."

Ryan's siblings laughed. Neal agreed, "My brother is finally right about something. Mom, you need to be with Will."

Ryan smiled at Donna. "I have great nursing care, and you need a well-deserved break. Now, Mother, go and make arrangements for a trip to Atlanta. Will cannot have a homecoming without you."

Deborah's other children voiced their blessing and asked when they would get to meet Will.

"Will and I want you to meet as soon as possible. He has two children, Katie and Todd. Todd was helpful in making arrangements for my quick return home after I got Neal's call about Ryan. You will love Will; he is a wonderful man. He owns a home improvement business, so I'll be moving south when we marry."

Megan said, "Mother, we want you to be happy. You've always been there for us."

Deborah's eyes welled up with tears. God made the way for her to tell her children. She was thankful for their love and encouragement. Deborah picked up her purse and notebook and left to call the man she loved.

"Will, I'm coming to Atlanta."

"Deborah, is it true?"

"Yes, I'll be there as fast as I can pack."

"When did you decide this?"

"It wasn't me; it was my children. God made an opportunity for me to tell them about us, and they all feel I should be with you."

"What about Ryan?"

"The doctor is satisfied with his progress and said he's well enough to be moved to another facility for therapy. It was on Ryan's insistence that I be with you for your homecoming. Will, God is always right on time."

"Let me know when your flight arrives, and I'll have Todd meet you at the airport. I prayed you would be here for my discharge. God is good. I can't wait to see you."

Deborah drove home and booked her flight for the next morning. It would give her time to pack and take care of some pending bills. She laughed out loud when she realized she booked the ticket for a one-way trip. The only thing on her mind was seeing Will. She wasn't sure how long she would be in Atlanta, so she decided to make arrangements for the return trip after she got there. She was excited, anticipating seeing Will well and walking. She knew she wouldn't be getting any sleep with the thought of being with him again.

Deborah packed her laptop, as she felt Will would still need plenty of rest, and she also had several hours of flying time to fill. There had been much less time to write after Ryan regained consciousness, but now she could concentrate on the neglected novel.

Neal called. "Mother, would you like me to take you to the airport?"

"Yes, but I'd like to stop by to see Ryan before we leave." Deborah didn't feel guilty leaving him now. It was comforting to know he had Donna.

Going south was going to be a pleasant change for Deborah; it was late September, and the weather was turning colder in New Jersey. She was looking forward to Georgia's warm climate.

Chapter Seventeen

odd's three-year-old twins begged to ride to the airport when they heard Deborah was arriving and was going to be their new grandmother. It was hard to contain their excitement as they waited near the baggage area. When Todd saw Deborah, he waved for her to join them.

"We are so happy you are able to be here when Dad comes home." The twins pushed each other to be the first one to greet the special passenger.

"So which one is David and which is Daniel?" Deborah questioned.

Daniel looked up at her and said, "I'm Daniel. Are you going to marry our grandpa?"

Deborah smiled, nodded her head yes, and then hugged each one. Todd was a little embarrassed at Daniel's boldness, but he was pleased at Deborah's response.

As they approached the parking lot, Deborah noticed a man with a cane standing by Todd's car. As she walked toward him, she saw it was Will. Deborah ran to him and fell into his arms.

"Will, how did you get released so early?"

"Todd picked me up this morning. I got approval from the center to meet your flight. When the doctor heard I was meeting my fiancée, he was thrilled to sign my discharge papers. That reminds me of something I need to do." Will reached into his jacket pocket and pulled out a small box. As he opened it he said, "Let's make this official. Deborah, you opened my heart again, will you marry me?"

Deborah's eyes glistened with tears of joy. "Will, yes, I'll be yours forever."

The twins started to yell and jump up and down. Deborah and Will were delighted at their enthusiasm. Todd gave Deborah a kiss on the cheek and said, "I'll look forward to calling you mother, if you won't mind?"

"Todd, I couldn't think of a better name."

Deborah pulled out her cell phone and called Ryan. Neal was at the hospital, so they both heard the news. Deborah handed the phone to Will to speak with them, and they showered Will with words of approval and love. He was touched by their acceptance and told them he was anxious to meet them. Megan was just as overjoyed when Deborah called her with the news and wished them God's blessing on their engagement. Deborah couldn't imagine being happier. She turned to Will and asked, "Will Katie be at the house?"

Will's countenance dropped. "Deborah, I haven't mentioned Katie in our conversations for a reason. She has never gotten over the incident in the hospital."

"Oh no, Will, how terrible. Why didn't you tell me?"

"I thought she would have accepted the situation by the time you returned. Jamie and Susan have both spoken with her, and she said she's not upset with me, but she's not sure she can accept another woman in my life. Of course, it doesn't affect how I feel. She will just have to face the fact that we are in love."

"Will, I want her to approve of us. It isn't easy to start a new life with a family member being excluded. I should have known. I thought she had dealt with her feelings."

"Deborah, I'm sorry. I wanted this day to be perfect for you. It is for me."

"Will, your daughter needs us. She's been in a shell too long. I want her to have an important part in our family."

"It won't be easy. Can we just enjoy your visit?"

"Will, I want to, but I need to speak with Susan and Jamie to see if there's a way I can change Katie's mind about us."

"She's a very stubborn girl. I don't want you to be hurt."

"You're going to be my husband, and I'm looking forward to marrying you. Katie can't spoil that; I just want to include her in our happiness."

Will pulled Deborah's shoulder toward him and kissed her on the cheek. "Katie isn't the only one with a stubborn streak. I love you too much to try to stop you."

As they pulled to the front of the house, Betsy ran out to greet them. She couldn't help herself when she saw Will and threw her arms around him to welcome him home. She then reached to hug Deborah and told her how tickled she was for them. Betsy noticed the ring and held her again.

Deborah asked, "Todd, when am I going to meet Jamie?"

"She had an appointment she couldn't cancel, but she will join us later." Deborah and Will went inside and down the hallway leading to the high porch. Betsy met them with two tall glasses of sweet tea. They both smiled at the sight of the glasses. It reminded them of the tea they shared in Montana.

As Deborah looked out at the garden below, she said to Will, "It might be nice to be married in the spring between the two magnolia trees. They should be in bloom then." Will beamed at her suggestion. It had been his desire to be married in the garden. It was the place that gave him a sense of fulfillment and tranquility.

Jamie returned and went out to join them. "Dad, it's wonderful to have you finally home, and you must be Deborah. We're thrilled to have you with us. You apparently have made Dad very happy. Congratulations on your engagement."

Todd walked through the French doors leading to the porch and interrupted. "Has Jamie told you the news? We're going to have another baby."

Deborah reached to embrace them both. "Congratulations, what a special surprise."

Will couldn't restrain his tears. He grabbed Todd and held him tight. "This is one of the happiest days of my life." He hugged Jamie, and he then clasped Deborah's hand.

"Now may not be the time, but we have some other news. Jamie and I have found a house in Roswell. With our growing family, we'll need the extra room. It won't be ready until spring, but we thought you should know you'll have the house to yourselves."

"It's understandable you want your own place, but you don't have to leave just because I'll be living here," Deborah stated.

"Even though it will be an adjustment for me, it will work with the plans Deborah and I have been discussing about a May wedding in the garden," Will said.

"What a wonderful idea. I'll be glad to help you with any of the preparations," offered Jamie.

Deborah responded, "I would welcome your help, and with planning a time for our families to meet."

Todd spoke up, and suggested having a large Thanksgiving gathering.

"I love the idea. Now I just have to convince my family to fly to Atlanta for the holiday."

Deborah excused herself and called Susan. She was anxious to see if Susan had any idea as to how she may speak with Katie. "Hello, Susan, it's Deborah."

"This is a pleasant surprise. Are you calling from New Jersey?"

"Actually, I'm here at Will's house. I wanted to know if you had time for lunch this week; there's something I need to discuss with you."

Susan was curious, as there was timidity in Deborah's voice. "Anything wrong?"

"Nothing really. Will and I are officially engaged, and he gave me a beautiful ring, but I want to reach out to Katie while I'm visiting and would like your opinion on how to go about it."

Susan knew how much it meant to Deborah to connect with Katie. She also knew how adamant Katie was about her father not marrying again. "I'd be glad to have lunch with you but my suggestion is to just give her a little time—she'll come around."

"Well, I would feel better if we discussed her feelings. Will and I are going to try to have both families meet for Thanksgiving. We also want you and Robert to join us."

"We would be delighted to come, and if you need extra bedrooms for your family, they are more than welcome to stay with us." They made plans for lunch before Deborah rejoined the others. Jamie and Todd suggested celebrating their news about the new baby and their father's engagement by going out for dinner.

"That is an excellent suggestion," Will agreed.

Jamie slipped away and called to invite Katie but didn't mention the engagement or Deborah's presence in Atlanta. Katie agreed and told her sister-in-law she would meet them at the restaurant. Jamie felt she needed to break the news to Todd.

"Jamie, what were you thinking? You know how crazed my sister gets around Deborah."

"It's about time Katie grows up and realizes her daddy is going to get married whether she likes it or not."

"But tonight was supposed to be a celebration, and I'm not sure Katie will be the life of the party."

"Well, the sooner Katie gets used to the idea, the better. Promise me you won't say anything to your father about Katie joining us."

"I promise. I don't want to be the bearer of that bad news."

Todd had no idea how his sister would react when she saw Deborah. He didn't want to upset Jamie, as she was so happy about the new baby, so he reluctantly kept quiet. Todd whispered a prayer that Katie wouldn't cause a scene embarrassing their father.

Chapter Eighteen

The twins crawled into the back section of their father's Ford Expedition. Deborah and Will occupied the middle, as Jamie and Todd took their seats in front. Will took Deborah by the hand and squeezed her fingers lightly, feeling the engagement ring. "I'm so glad you got to come for my discharge. I've missed you more than you can imagine."

Will was thrilled at the events of the day, having a new grandchild was just the icing on the cake for his return home. He looked at Deborah, her lips curved upward, smiling with so much love and contentment; there was nothing that could ruin this day, Will thought.

Todd stopped near the front door of the restaurant, so his father wouldn't have to walk from the parking lot. Will was still getting accustomed to walking with a cane, and the doctor said it would take a few more weeks to get back to his normal physical activity. The restaurant was crowded, as it usually was, and Will told his son that he would see the hostess about a table while Todd parked the car. It was then Todd knew he had to divulge the secret. "Dad, we need a table for seven."

"There are only six of us, Todd; Jamie hasn't had the baby yet."

Jamie felt she should answer Will, since it had been her idea, "Katie will be with us tonight."

Will knew he should be glad to hear the news of his daughter joining them for the family celebration, but he just looked at Jamie with a somber stare.

"It's a great idea. Katie will realize we want her with us to celebrate the happy occasions," Deborah said hesitantly. She was trying to calm the agitation Will seemed to be having over the news.

The prayer she prayed only hours before was being answered, she would be seeing Katie much sooner than she expected, and she wanted the time spent with her to be pleasant. Deborah knew there was a great possibility it may not be as she wanted, but she was determined to make her best effort for peace between them.

As everyone except Todd exited the car, Will suggested they shouldn't tell Katie of the engagement if they wanted to enjoy their dinner.

Jamie loved her father-in-law but felt he coddled his daughter. "Why do you allow Katie's opinions to dictate everything?" Jamie knew she was being confrontational, but she was sick of her sister-in-law's domineering ways.

"Jamie, I think it would be better if we just don't mention it tonight."

Deborah was disappointed not to be able to share their news with Katie. She slipped the engagement ring from her finger without anyone noticing and opened her purse. Deborah was careful to put the ring in the zippered pocket so it wouldn't be misplaced as the hostess showed them to a table in the center of the room.

Todd met his sister on the way into the restaurant. "Congratulations, Todd. Jamie told me your good news." Todd just grinned and thanked her. "Where are Jamie and the boys?"

"They're inside with Dad and Deborah."

"Deborah! Jamie didn't mention she was in town."

"Look, Sis, she came to see Dad since he was released today. Don't upset him."

"You of all people know how I feel about her. How could you do this to me?"

"It is always about you. Why can't you think about someone else once in a while?"

"If it wasn't for disappointing Jamie, I'd leave right now."

"Just be careful not to embarrass our father. Heaven knows why, but he loves you."

Todd saw Jamie gesture for them to come to the table. "After you, sister dear," Todd said as he stepped aside to allow Katie to walk in front of him. Jamie stood and walked toward Katie. She reached out and hugged her, and Katie whispered in her ear, "Why did you invite me, knowing she was here?" Jamie just smiled and whispered back, "You are part of this family; please be nice for Dad's sake."

Katie greeted her father and said it was good that he was finally able to go home. Will uttered, "Katie, you remember Deborah, don't you?" How could she not remember the woman who had pushed her way into her father's life? Katie wanted to run away, anywhere, but knew she had to compose herself, "Hello, Mrs. Miller. So nice to see you again."

Deborah knew Katie's greeting was insincere, but she wasn't going to let anything ruin the opportunity to spend time with Will's daughter. It was her belief that God could turn things around, and she could be the friend Katie needed. "Hello, Katie, it is a pleasure to see you again. I was in a rush to get home the last time I saw you. I apologize if you were surprised by my exit."

Katie knew she should answer her father's friend. After all, she had the advantage; Deborah was apologizing to her. "Yes, how is your son?"

"He's doing well; thank you for asking."

Will wasn't sure what was happening, but he felt the necessity to interrupt and end the tension.

"Everyone sit down, so we can order."

"Aunt Katie, come sit between us," said one of the twins.

The conversation changed to the subject of another niece or nephew for Katie to spoil. The twins were well behaved and hadn't been very talkative, but as the waiter asked if they wanted dessert, Daniel said, "Grandma Deborah, what do you want?"

Todd almost choked on the coffee he was drinking.

"She's not your grandmother, Daniel," Katie remarked.

"She's going to be; show Aunt Katie your pretty ring."

"What!" Katie's face was beet red. "Dad, is he right?"

"We might as well tell you the truth; you were going to find out sooner or later. Yes, Katie, I've asked Deborah to marry me."

"This is not what I wanted to hear. Thank you for dinner, but I'm leaving now." Katie picked up her purse and hurried to the entrance. She almost knocked a man over as she pushed the door open.

Jamie started to run after her, but Will said, "Just let her leave; she won't listen to you."

The reaction of Katie's genuine outrage surprised Deborah. It was going to be even more difficult to win her over than Deborah imagined.

"I'm sorry for inviting her," said Jamie. "I thought it might help her to spend some time with you, Deborah."

Will paid the bill, and they stood to leave. He reached over, and grabbed Deborah by the left hand. He expected to feel the ring on her finger. "Where is your ring?"

"I took it off before we came into the restaurant. I didn't want Katie to see it, since we weren't going to tell her."

"Just because I didn't want to tell Katie didn't mean for you not to wear your ring. You don't ever have to take it off again. You shouldn't have felt the necessity to remove it from Katie's view."

"That was fine. Now that she knows, it doesn't matter. I just wish she hadn't been kept in the dark again. She shouldn't have heard about our engagement from the boys. If I were in her position, I would be hurt too."

Everyone was silent in the car. The twins were exhausted and fell asleep.

When they arrived home, Todd carried the boys upstairs to bed, and Jamie went to see that they were dressed in their pajamas. Will told Deborah he wanted to find some papers that he needed from the library and to make herself comfortable.

Feeling slightly abandoned, she walked to the kitchen to get a drink of water. She wasn't really thirsty, but it kept her busy until Will could join her.

Betsy heard someone in the kitchen and came bursting through the door leading to her room. "I thought I heard someone in the house. May I get you something, Deborah?"

"No, thank you, Betsy; I just wanted a glass of water."

Betsy sensed something in Deborah's voice that didn't sound like the woman she had met several months before. "Deborah, is everything all right?"

"Not really, Betsy. You're very perceptive."

"Is there anything I can do?"

"It's really nothing. Katie met us for dinner, and she wasn't very enthused at her father being engaged."

"Oh, that child has a way of making everyone miserable. Don't take anything she says very seriously. I think she acts the way she does just to get attention."

"I wanted all of our children to be excited for us, but it's very evident that isn't happening. Maybe we should have waited. I didn't anticipate the problem it would cause."

"Deborah, you're the best thing that's happened to Mr. Dougherty since his wife died. I see a difference in the way he acts; it is like the old times when he was happy-go-lucky. Don't let Katie bother you. But there I go again, talking too much."

"Thank you, Betsy. That's nice to hear from someone so close to the family."

Will walked in and said, "There you are. I wondered where you had gone. I told Todd that we are going fishing tomorrow on Lake Lanier. He is going to check on the stores in the morning and pick us up about eleven o'clock. You do like fishing, don't you?"

"Yes, that sounds like fun."

Betsy said, "You'll enjoy the lake; it is so pretty and peaceful during the week. Now, if you'll excuse me, I need to get my beauty sleep, although you know it doesn't seem to help. See you in the morning."

"Betsy, may we have some of your blueberry waffles for breakfast?" Will asked.

"Sure you can, Mr. Dougherty. Good night now."

It was almost in unison that Will and Deborah said, "Good night."

Just then, Jamie walked through the kitchen door. "Deborah, I'm very sorry tonight turned out the way it did, please forgive me."

"Jamie, it wasn't your fault Katie reacted the way she did; I'm not going to hold this against her, she needs us.'"

"Thank you. Todd said to tell you good night. I'll see you in the morning." Jamie turned around and the door closed behind her.

Will's mood became doleful. "I'm sorry you experienced Katie's indefensible behavior."

"It may have been our fault for not considering the effect it would have on her. After all, she hadn't dealt with my surprise entrance into your hospital room. It must feel like I'm stealing you from her."

"Katie is a grown woman, and it's about time she starts acting the part. I'm not going to excuse her behavior tonight. Maybe Jamie was right about me allowing her to control my life. What did she say? Katie dictates everything? I've spoiled her since her mother died and overlooked her possessiveness."

"Will, don't overreact; we need to consider how we can reach her. She seemed emotionally devastated."

"You're much more forgiving of her than I am. We've had a busy day, so let's retire early. I'm already missing my naps."

"All right. I'm pretty exhausted myself." Deborah was relieved there would be no more conversation about the dinner that turned disastrous. She was anxious to spend time in prayer for Katie. In his current state, Deborah wasn't sure Will would be seeking God's answer for his daughter tonight. They walked up the stairway to the second floor, and before retiring to the master bedroom, Will kissed Deborah good night.

Deborah continued down the hallway to the guest room. She was determined to pray until Katie agreed to come for the family gathering at Thanksgiving, but she wasn't expecting the consequences of those prayers.

Chapter Nineteen

There was a bright light shining through the window in Deborah's room. She jumped out of bed and pulled the drapes open completely. Basking in the warmth of the sun, she took a deep breath and felt so fortunate to be in Georgia and not in cold Mount Holly. She thought about Will saying he would take her to the lake and decided to dress in a denim skirt and plaid blouse. She had packed the casual outfit knowing how much Will liked to fish and felt she should be prepared for the boat ride mentioned the previous night.

Yes, the previous night, Deborah thought. She wondered how Katie was doing. It was a scene Deborah hadn't expected to encounter.

There was a knock at her door, and she walked across the room to answer it. Jamie was standing alone in the hallway. "May I come in?"

"Of course you may." Deborah could see the strain on her face and knew she was still concerned with the way Katie left the restaurant.

"Deborah, I am so sorry about last night. I know I've apologized, but it was my idea to ask Katie, and I didn't realize how awful it would turn out."

"Don't worry about me. I can understand how she must feel—another woman taking her father's affection. There must be some way of making her understand that her father will always love her, and that won't change. I would like to get to know her and someday have her accept me as her mother."

"Oh, I really wish that were possible, but I've known her for about five years, and she can be obstinate. You shouldn't get your hopes up."

Deborah reached over and touched Jamie's shoulder. "Well, we're not going to worry about that now. I'm getting hungry. Do you think Betsy will have the waffles ready soon?"

"I was downstairs earlier, and she had coffee brewing, so I'm sure it won't be long before breakfast is served. Dad was reading the paper in the library when I came up to speak with you."

"Then I guess we should find him."

"You go on ahead. I want to check on the twins."

Deborah descended the large staircase and thought how fortunate she was going to be as the "lady" of the house.

The library was located at the bottom of the staircase, and Will peered over his newspaper as Deborah entered the room. "You're up, that's great. I see you've dressed for our fishing trip. I can't wait to show you Lake Lanier. Todd will have to go with us to steer the boat, but it shouldn't be too long before I can take it out myself. He should be here after breakfast."

"How far is it to this special lake?"

"It's about half an hour to our boat dock. This time of year, the lake is not as crowded as it is in summer. It's known as the recreational playground for the wealthy of Atlanta. Weekends are normally crammed with jet skis, speedboats pulling inflatable tubes, and houseboats. It isn't ideal fishing conditions in the middle of the lake when it's packed with boaters, but there are over six hundred miles of shoreline, so there are always quiet, little inlets for fishing."

"I didn't realize it was so big."

"The entire lake covers about thirty-eight thousand acres. The Buford Dam, built by the US Army Corps of Engineers in 1956, created it. It is spread across five different counties. During the 1996 Summer Olympics, the lake was used for the rowing and canoe sprint competitions. But the real purpose for the lake was flood control in Atlanta, hydroelectricity, and water supply to the region."

"I'm surprised; I never knew there was a large lake near Atlanta."

"Actually, there are several."

Betsy interrupted their conversation to say breakfast was being served. Will asked, "Would you please pack a picnic lunch for us to take to the lake?"

"Of course," answered Betsy.

He folded his paper and laid it on the desk, then took Deborah by the arm. They walked into the large dining room where Deborah had eaten dinner with Todd several months before. The table was a little less formal, with just one side of the table set for the family.

The twins were anxious to get outside to play, so they hurried through breakfast and asked if they could be excused. Jamie smiled, and warned them to be careful. The adults sipped coffee and made small talk, trying to avoid conversation about the dinner with Katie. Todd came into the room and greeted everyone. "I see you are all awake."

Will brushed his napkin over his mouth and said, "If you want to do any fishing today, we should probably be on our way. It might be good to take your jacket; it can be cold on the water."

Betsy entered the dining room carrying the picnic basket and said, "Bring us lots of fish for dinner."

Deborah told the men she would meet them by the front door in a few minutes. She smiled at Jamie and told her she would love to have a conversation with her later that evening.

Jamie said, "I'd enjoy that very much. I'll plan to put the boys to bed early." Though she hoped Katie wouldn't be part of their conversation.

Chapter Twenty

As they drove to the lake, Will pointed out the various exits of Route 400 and the shopping areas, well hidden by the trees lining the roadway. He wanted to make Deborah aware of the numerous stores near his home.

When they reached the dock, Todd pulled into the parking area. Will led Deborah to a pier and gestured to an imposing houseboat. "That's our ride."

"Will, you didn't say you owned a houseboat."

"It's so much better for a day of fishing. We've got all the facilities we need onboard."

"What other surprises do you have for me?"

"There is nothing more at this moment."

Todd laughed and got behind the wheel. "Are you ready to go?"

"Yes, I'm really looking forward to this trip."

Will told Deborah about the parks and campgrounds available along the banks of Lake Lanier and pointed to the boat ramps for the public to use.

"This is incredible; I can see why you enjoy coming here."

After slowly touring the lake and enjoying the lunch prepared by Betsy, Todd dropped anchor and got his fishing rod. He went to the opposite side of the boat from where his father was seated and pulled a chair near the side railing.

Will handed Deborah an extra fishing rod that he kept onboard and watched as she surprised him with her casting technique. "You have fished before, haven't you?"

Deborah smiled and said, "I'm certainly not a novice."

The couple enjoyed their time on the water but were a little disappointed that they only caught a few small fish. Todd hadn't done much better, so he joined them and asked, "Are you ready to leave?"

"I suppose. Deborah and I weren't very successful, so I'll call home and let them know we're on our way." Will pulled his cell phone from his pocket. "Jamie, we just finished fishing and should be home in about an hour. Tell Betsy we didn't catch enough fish for dinner."

"Thanks for calling, Dad. See you soon."

After Todd pulled into the dock and let his father and Deborah disembark, he secured the boat and met them at the car. "Well, Deborah, how did you like our lake?"

"I loved it—it's so peaceful—and I've never fished from a houseboat before."

"Yes, my father enjoys the best of everything now, and I'm glad he does. But it isn't always that peaceful on the lake."

Traffic was heavy as they made their way down Route 400, and it took them longer than the usual half hour to get home. When they arrived, the twins were waiting for them on the porch. "Daddy, did you catch a big fish?"

"Not today, son."

"Momma said dinner is almost ready."

They walked into the house, and Betsy said, "You're right on time; go to the dining room, and I'll get the food on the table."

Deborah loved the way Betsy was so informal. She was glad she would have her full-time to help take care of the immense home.

After dinner, Jamie got the boys ready for bed, and then looked for Deborah, who was sitting on the high porch with Will. "Deborah, the boys are in bed now, if you'd like to have our talk."

"Will, do you mind us using the library? I'd like to speak with Jamie."

"By all means; use it as long as you need to."

Deborah and Jamie walked into the house and down the hallway to the library. They talked about the many chores of the house and what Betsy's responsibilities were. "I'm happy you agreed to help me with the wedding plans. I will need someone here in Atlanta to oversee some of the tasks," Deborah said. "I know I can count on Will, but it's nice to have a woman who understands the importance of having every detail planned in advance. I have another request, though. Please help me pray that Katie will join the family at Thanksgiving. The whole idea is to have all the family members meet, and I wouldn't want her to be the only one missing."

"Sure, Deborah. I know how difficult she can be at times, but there is a side of her few people see. She is so sweet and kind to my boys, and I know she really loves them."

"That is the Katie I want to get to know."

With the conversation of Katie behind them, the two women laughed and talked for more than an hour. Will and Todd couldn't take their absence any longer and went to the library. "Can we come in to say good night?"

"I didn't realize we had been in here so long," said Deborah.

"This man needs some sleep." Will chuckled.

"All right, we're finished exchanging ideas for having the wedding in the garden. It helps to have another woman's viewpoint, and since Jamie has offered to help, I wanted to get her advice."

They walked to the upstairs hallway and told each other good night. Will pulled Deborah into his arms and kissed her. "I'll see you in the morning."

The rest of the week was spent making guest lists and checking for caterers in the area. Will took Deborah to a local hotel where they reserved a banquet room for the rehearsal dinner. Will also had a friend who was a professional photographer, and they called him to do the wedding photos. A florist was contacted, and they chose white roses to be used in the bouquets and the arch Deborah wanted between the magnolia trees. Everything seemed to be going smoothly when she left Atlanta. It was only the first week in October when she arrived home, and she knew she would be returning for Thanksgiving, but in the meantime, she planned to e-mail instructions to Jamie for the many unfinished wedding details.

Deborah was looking forward to her children meeting the special man she would spend the rest of her life with, although she felt Thanksgiving without Katie was unacceptable. It was going to be her fervent prayer for Katie to attend the family gathering.

Chapter Twenty-One

With the holiday a little more than a month away, Deborah phoned her children to make the arrangements for Thanksgiving in Atlanta. She called her daughter first, knowing Megan would be up early to get the girls ready for school, and Megan was thrilled. It would work with her plans to take the children to Disney World. They could spend the holiday in Atlanta and fly to Florida on Friday. When Deborah told Megan about Susan's offer, Megan agreed it would be better for her family to stay with the Bennings, since they would only need a room for two nights.

Deborah called Neal's office and asked if he could fly to Atlanta with Ryan on the Tuesday before Thanksgiving. Neal wasn't very receptive and responded, "Mom, it's a busy time for my company; don't count on me leaving early, but I promise to be at the family dinner on Thursday." She was somewhat disappointed by his lack of enthusiasm but felt it wouldn't deter her mission to get her family to Georgia to meet Will.

Still wearing her pajamas, she dressed to visit Ryan. She had been concerned he might not be able to travel by the end of November. As she entered his room, Donna greeted her with a hug and Deborah felt how fortunate her son was to have the love of such a beautiful Christian woman.

"Ryan is looking much better than when I left." Deborah felt their love must have been aiding the healing process.

When she told Ryan and Donna about the Thanksgiving gathering, Donna said, "I'm sorry, I'll have to decline the invitation, my plans with my family are unchangeable. But I know how important it is for Ryan to meet Will, so he must go."

Deborah asked the doctor if he felt Ryan could make the trip. The doctor was pleased with Ryan's progress; he believed Ryan would be able to travel with the assistance of a wheelchair.

Neal called his mother, "I checked with the office, and I have to work until Wednesday afternoon, but you can count on me to take you to the airport. I'll make arrangements to leave the office before your flight to help with Ryan."

With the preliminary arrangements made, Deborah felt the family dinner just might occur.

Chapter Twenty-Two

Visits to the rehab center, writing, and long hours on the phone with Will made the days pass quickly. Before she knew it, she was packing for the family holiday. She had made great progress on her manuscript and knew she wouldn't feel guilty taking a few days off in Atlanta.

The sun was shining, but the temperature was bone-chilling as Neal drove Deborah and Ryan through Philadelphia. "We won't need our heavy coats in Atlanta," Deborah declared. "You will love the weather."

Although Ryan had done remarkably well in the previous weeks and was maneuvering his wheelchair with ease, it was arduous getting the wheelchair in and out of the car. Deborah was glad Neal was able to assist her. When they reached the airport, Neal found a parking space close to the terminal and helped them check their bags. An attendant for the airline saw them obtaining their boarding passes and volunteered to push the chair to their departure gate. Having his help, Deborah breathed a little easier.

In Atlanta, Will understood he couldn't handle the luggage and Ryan's wheelchair, so he asked Todd to ride with him to the airport. They arrived shortly before the plane touched down, so Will decided to get a cup of coffee as they waited.

The coats they had been wearing were now on their arms as Deborah entered the baggage claim area with Ryan. Her mind was focused on getting the bags, when she got a tap on the shoulder. Turning around to see who was trying to get her attention, Deborah grabbed Todd's shoulder and then hugged him. "What are you doing here?"

"We were surprised you didn't see us sitting at the restaurant in the connecting corridor. Dad thought I should come and help you."

"Is he here?"

"Yes, right over there." Todd was pointing in the direction of the hallway in front of the baggage area.

Slowly limping toward her, Will waved enthusiastically. Deborah forgot about retrieving her luggage and ran to meet him. Will wrapped his arms around her and kissed her with fervor; it was proof to her she was truly missed. There was nothing to make her doubt his love ever again.

"We're ready to leave," Todd announced as the couple walked toward him.

"I'm sorry, I was not there to retrieve everything and introduce you to my son," Deborah told Todd.

"Ryan pointed out the bags. I noticed you two were preoccupied," Todd said as he grinned at Ryan.

"Todd and I have had quite a conversation waiting on you two," Ryan joked.

Will extended his hand to Ryan, "I am very glad to meet you. I've prayed many prayers for you, young man. How are you feeling after your flight?"

"I'm a little tired but doing great."

"That's really good news to hear."

Will and Ryan became instant friends. They had an immediate bond, having dealt with the effects of their accidents and the need for a long recovery. Will was able to relate to Ryan, and hoped he would find it as easy to interact with Deborah's other children.

When they finally arrived at Will's home, Ryan was amazed at the beauty of the landscaping. "Mom, I agree with you, this would make a magnificent setting for the wedding." During their stay, Ryan enjoyed sitting on the high porch and viewing the garden below.

Megan took the children out of school a day early, arriving in Atlanta on Wednesday afternoon. Deborah's granddaughters found instant playmates in Todd's twins. On the tour of his home, Will won Megan and Jason over too; they were fascinated with his southern mansion.

All seemed to be going well. The Lord answered Deborah's prayers, and Katie had even agreed to come for the weekend. Katie would stay in the extra room in the west wing with Todd's family. Deborah and her sons would occupy the two extra bedrooms in the east wing near Will. A personal elevator had been added to the stairs in the kitchen during Sherry's illness, and it allowed Ryan access to the second floor.

Since Katie worked in downtown Atlanta, Will asked if she would pick up Neal from the airport on Wednesday evening. She was much closer, and it was a ploy to guarantee her presence for the family gathering. Katie reluctantly agreed, but not before plotting to use the opportunity to uncover all she could about Deborah from her son.

Chapter Twenty-Three

Katie stood restless, tapping her toes, inside the terminal, vexed by the thought of the passenger soon to arrive. The idea of a stepbrother sickened her. She only agreed to give Neal a ride to glean information she needed to sabotage her father's marriage. Just then, a tall slender man with ebony hair and baby blue eyes stepped through the gate. Katie was breathless. Her heart began pounding. She couldn't understand what was transpiring. The man was heart-stoppingly handsome, but Katie wondered why the stranger would evoke the feelings she was experiencing. He walked past her and disappeared. Katie continued to wait for Neal, but he didn't seem to be on the flight; infuriated, she had him paged.

Katie had her back turned when a man's voice said, "Are you Katie?" Katie turned to stand before the man who had just taken her breath away. She managed to mumble, "Yes, I'm Katie."

"Hi, I'm Neal. You're cuter than I pictured," he teased.

Katie was at a loss for words. Flustered, she started fussing with her strawberry blonde hair, wondering why she hadn't combed it before leaving work. This was not going to be easy, she mused. She felt her face flush as she hoped her clothes weren't wrinkled after a day in the office, but he had said she was cute. Now it seemed she had no control over the situation.

As they walked to the car, Neal asked if there was a mall nearby. He had forgotten to bring a tie for Sunday's church service.

"North Point Mall is near the house; if you'd like, we can stop there," answered Katie.

"Great, and forgive me but I'm starving. The airline snacks aren't very filling, and I haven't had dinner. Is there a good restaurant near the mall?"

"Several, but if you like cheesecake I know the perfect place," remarked Katie.

Neal was delighted at her recommendation of the Cheesecake Factory. "That's excellent; we also have them in the North."

The idea of being alone with this gorgeous man was quite appealing; though chatting with Neal was just a little unnerving; he made her pulse race. Despite her emotions, she found herself enjoying his company and the planned interrogation had been forgotten.

At the mall, Neal found a tie, and then the couple walked through the parking lot to the restaurant. They talked for a few hours and were surprised when the waiter told them the restaurant would be closing. Neal's cell phone rang, and his mother wanted to know if anything was wrong. As they hurried to the car, Katie and Neal laughed, realizing they had lost all track of time.

"I guess we're in trouble for being out late," Neal joked. "I didn't want to make a bad impression with my mother's fiancé."

"We'll be there shortly. Dad is very forgiving, but I hope your mother doesn't hold this against me."

"Mom would never do such a thing. She's the sweetest, kindest person I know, and I'm not just saying that because she's my mother. She has helped others in so many ways. I thought she should be nominated for sainthood."

Katie was perplexed. Had she met the same woman? Maybe she had prejudged her, as Susan and Jamie said. Katie didn't want to believe them but knew she also hadn't given Deborah a chance to prove what kind of person she truly was. Katie knew she needed to keep an open mind; after all, she was Neal's mother.

Will and Deborah were waiting at the door as Katie and Neal ran up the front stairs to meet them.

Katie said sheepishly, "Dad, we stopped by the mall and got something to eat."

"It was my fault, sir. I had forgotten a tie and was famished," Neal interjected.

Deborah laughed, "You two sound like teens caught out after curfew." Deborah moved close to Katie and reached out her hands to hug her. "Katie, it's good to see you again."

Katie saw Deborah's outstretched arms and felt very uncomfortable. Will gave Katie a long stare, which didn't help her apprehension. She decided she better at least meet Deborah halfway. Katie reached over and gave Deborah a brief hug. It appeared as an awkward response. Deborah turned to Neal, and embraced him while Katie retreated to the car for her suitcase. Neal shook Will's hand then turned and descended the stairs to retrieve his luggage.

"What was that, Katie?"

"What do you mean?"

"Do you and my mother have issues?"

"Not really, but I guess we didn't meet under the best of circumstances." Katie tried to make light of her true feelings. She liked Neal and didn't want to leave the wrong impression; he seemed very close to his mother.

When they were inside, Katie ascended the stairs and disappeared down the hallway. Will and Deborah showed Neal to the kitchen, where they had a pot of coffee brewing.

"I'm really not thirsty. We had several cups of coffee over dinner. If you don't mind showing me to my room, we can get acquainted tomorrow," said Neal.

Deborah stood speechless. It wasn't like Neal to be rude. She sensed something must have been bothering him, and Deborah wondered if Katie had been contentious. She knew it had been an imposition for her to pick up Neal. Deborah was curious as to what kept them out so late.

Betsy appeared, and Will asked her to show Neal to the bedroom he would be sharing with Ryan.

With Neal out of the kitchen, Will shook his head and told Deborah he was wrong sending Katie to the airport. "She has a habit of upsetting people. I'm sorry she was so cold toward you," said Will.

"It will take time, but I'm not giving up on her. It was Neal I was concerned about. He is never rude."

They agreed they needed to pray for God's help for the family to enjoy the rest of the weekend. Since it was after midnight, they said good night and retired to their rooms.

Deborah arose early and went to the kitchen where Betsy was busy making pies and preparing the turkey for the oven. They worked together on dinner until the family began to awaken; Betsy then changed her priority and started breakfast. Jamie joined them and showed Deborah where the dishes and silverware were kept. Betsy welcomed the help, as she wasn't accustomed to such a large group. The smell of brewing coffee brought Will downstairs.

Katie made an appearance in the kitchen and announced, "Don't set a place for me. I won't be here for breakfast, but I'll be here for dinner."

Will was livid. He was hoping she could spend time with Deborah and her family, while they were in Atlanta.

As Katie was leaving, Todd came down the stairs. "Aren't you staying, Sis?"

"I've forgotten some things, and I need to return home. I'll be back." Todd gave her a smirk and shook his head in disapproval. He didn't know Katie wanted to be a little more presentable for Neal. The wardrobe she had packed wasn't very flattering. It would also allow time for her father to cool down about her distant behavior toward Deborah. She certainly didn't want him confronting her about the previous night. Megan, Jason, and their daughters met Katie on the front porch. They introduced themselves, and Katie promised to see them later.

With Megan and her family assembled, they all took their seats in the large dining room. Deborah was amazed at the size of the combined families. With Todd's new baby and Donna marrying Ryan, they would need a larger table next year.

After breakfast, the twins took Deborah's granddaughters out to the play area. Will had built a small park on the side of the house. Deborah was glad Todd would have a large yard to accommodate the swings and other playthings. Though the tree house would have to remain; it was just too enormous to move.

That afternoon, the children told embarrassing stories about their parents, and the house was filled with laughter. Deborah thought of Katie and what she was missing; this was the type of bonding Katie needed to feel a true connection to the family.

Will and Deborah were enjoying the company of their children and felt the transition of the families would be, for the most part, an easy one. It also helped that the children were grown and wouldn't be living at home.

Katie arrived shortly before dinner. Susan and Robert Benning had followed her up the driveway, and they entered the house together. Neal and Ryan were excited to see the Bennings and thanked them for the kindness shown to their mother.

Everyone was escorted into the beautifully decorated dining room, with late blooming flowers from Will's garden, and the china Sherry purchased in Japan adorning the table. The gold chargers and silverware complimented the gold rim on the plates. Deborah and Will sat on either end of the table, smiling at the feat they had accomplished in just over a month. The two families were together and having a good time. Will used the occasion to thank the Lord for each of them. Deborah was thrilled knowing she would be marrying a man with her convictions and love of God. She felt truly blessed.

Dinner was delicious, and everyone ate too much, as with most Thanksgiving feasts. The men retreated to the den for the football game, and the women gathered in the living room and shared the excitement of Jamie's pregnancy. Deborah felt it would be a good time to share the plans she and Will were making.

"I would like you all to be part of the wedding party," Deborah announced.

"You shouldn't plan on me," said Jamie. "I would love to be in the wedding, but I'll be in my final month. If I have another set of twins, they could arrive early."

"That's understandable, though I want you to feel included. My sister Nancy will be my matron of honor. Todd will be the best man. Jason, Ryan, and Neal will be our ushers. I thought Megan and Katie would be bridesmaids. I can ask Donna to take Jamie's place. We want our grandchildren involved, too. The twins will be ring bearers, and Sara, Valerie, and Kathleen can be flower girls."

Megan asked, "Why are you planning such a large wedding, Mom?"

"Will and I want it to be a celebration of our families, as well as our marriage."

"I think it's a wonderful idea. I'm excited for you both," said Jamie.

Deborah questioned, "Is everyone in agreement with what I've said?" Katie was very quiet and seemed distressed. "Katie, I thought you might walk with Neal. Are you all right with the idea?" Deborah wanted to hear Katie's approval verbally.

"Yes, whatever you decide. It's your wedding." Katie felt a little claustrophobic and excused herself. Jamie got up to follow her, but Deborah motioned to let her go.

Katie passed the den, and Neal noticed her walking toward the door. He followed her outside, without her knowledge. She quickly walked down the garden path beyond the magnolia trees to a bench hidden from view of the house; it had been her retreat when visiting her parents. It was a place to regroup when problems arose. Katie closed her eyes to consider why the wedding plans troubled her so much.

"May I sit down?"

Startled, Katie opened her eyes to see Neal standing in front of her. "Be my guest," she said smugly.

"You seem to have difficulty dealing with the family gathering," said Neal.

"Not really; it's just hard for me to accept my father marrying again."

"I assure you, he's getting a great lady," Neal teased.

Katie said nothing. Sitting close to Neal, she could feel her heart pounding. She wasn't sure how to control her feelings.

"Katie, I'm really attracted to you, and I'm not sure why. Yes, I do know why. You're beautiful, and I felt we really connected on the way from the airport. I don't want to add to your tension, but I learned through my brother's accident that we need to say what we feel before it's too late."

"Neal, you're the only one, recently, I've been able to enjoy spending time with. I do feel there is something special between us. My heart has never raced like this before." She couldn't believe those words came out of her mouth. "Did I say that out loud?"

Neal pulled Katie toward him and kissed her. She returned his kiss but then pulled away and said, "How will this ever work? You'll be my stepbrother. Life has always posed complications for me."

"We won't be blood related. It makes a huge difference. I do want to get to know you better."

"Neal, I've been rude to your mother. How can she possibly approve of us being together?"

"If she knows I have feelings for you, she'll have no problem with us. Have you ever spoken with her?"

"No, not really. Why do they need to have such a large wedding?"

"That is their business. You need to speak with my mother. She is a loving and understanding person. She would do anything for you."

"Everyone has accused me of misjudging her. I suppose they all can't be wrong. It must be me."

Neal placed a kiss on her forehead and asked her to show him the garden. They walked slowly through the rows of flowers and manicured bushes. Katie found peace in Neal's words. She was determined to change her feelings toward Deborah.

Deborah left the living room to have Betsy prepare some tea. Looking out the window toward the garden hoping to see Katie, she noticed Neal first and then observed Katie walking near him. Deborah was glad to see them together. After Wednesday night's incident, she hoped they would be friends.

Chapter Twenty-Four

Friday was a picture-perfect day. The weather was unseasonably warm and sunny. Todd planned to take his family, Neal, and Ryan to Stone Mountain Park, and Katie decided to join them.

Katie and Neal kept their distance so as not to reveal their attachment. Neal kept busy pushing Ryan around in the wheelchair and teasing with Todd's sons. They all took the tram ride to the top of the mountain to give Deborah's sons an up-close look at the carvings of the Confederate leaders on horseback and the panoramic view of Atlanta. It was quite a feat getting Ryan onto the rocks for a vantage point of the city. The skyscrapers and famous "King" and "Queen" buildings, which resemble chess pieces, were easily recognizable.

The train ride was much easier to maneuver for Ryan, and afterward, Neal and Katie took the twins miniature golfing.

While the children were gone, Will took Deborah for a driving tour of Alpharetta and Roswell. Deborah couldn't believe the many shopping areas available within a short distance of Will's home. The roads were crowded with holiday shoppers getting the special bargains of Black Friday. As they drove through North Point Mall, she spied the American Girl store, and Deborah knew her granddaughters would be thrilled to take their dolls to lunch and shop for their latest fashions and accessories.

Will drove Deborah through neighborhoods with massive homes. "I want you to be comfortable when we marry. I can't possibly expect you to live in a home I built for another woman. You can see there are plenty of beautiful houses for sale, or we can stay in my home until we can build our own."

"Will, I couldn't think of living anywhere but in the home you built. How could you leave your garden? Sherry will always be a part of you and your children. It's a beautiful home, and I wouldn't be content anywhere else. I haven't seen anything today as grand."

They went to a Louisiana-style seafood restaurant for dinner. Afterward, Will suggested, "We should probably go home and wait for the children."

"Yes, the twins should be worn out by now."

Will held Deborah's chair and helped her with her light jacket. They made it home long before the rest of the family.

David and Daniel came running through the front door, and talked nonstop about the fun they had. Jamie took them upstairs to put them to bed while the adults settled in around the kitchen table for coffee and leftover pumpkin pie.

The weekend was working out the way Will and Deborah had hoped.

Chapter Twenty-Five

The entire family went to the gold mine in Dahlonega, Georgia, on Saturday. It was famous for the saying, "There's gold in them there hills." Todd took his family in his car, and the others rode with Will.

The ride up Route 400 was fast paced but scenic, as the leaves were still colorful. Will promised Deborah's sons, "On the way back, I'll take you to Buford Dam. I'd also like to take the boat out tomorrow after church, so we can enjoy this unseasonably warm weather."

Ryan spoke up. "Don't plan on me for the boat trip, this wheelchair is a bit bulky."

"Wait until you see Will's boat," Deborah chuckled. "I don't think there will be a problem."

Upon arriving in Dahlonega, the family challenged one another to find the largest gold nugget at the mine. Jamie won the challenge. The gold was too small to really be called nuggets; even so, they had fun trying to win bragging rights. They strolled through the town with its quaint shops, and Deborah was able to find several souvenirs for her granddaughters.

They decided to eat at the area's famous Smith House. The old Victorian home, which had been converted into a restaurant, was a favorite among those living in the North Georgia mountains. It was also a tourist destination, with its homey Southern dishes and a room set apart to view an old gold mine within its walls. The service was home-style, the food served in large bowls for all to enjoy. The dinner included: black-eyed peas, fried okra, creamed corn, fried apples, and the best fried chicken Deborah had ever eaten.

On the drive back to Alpharetta, Deborah noticed the sign for Dawsonville, Sherry's hometown. She no longer felt threatened by Will's first wife. She was grateful for the love and care Sherry had given her family.

Will took a detour from 400 to Buford Dam and Lake Lanier. The rather short, narrow bridge over the water was a little scary, and the drop off for the dam was quite intimidating. It was dusk, and there was a beautiful reddish-orange sunset over the lake.

With a church service to attend the following morning, they went to their bedrooms shortly after returning home.

The family gathered at church, where Robert Benning preached an anointed message. He acknowledged Deborah and her sons during the service and made them feel like welcomed guests. Deborah felt indebted to the Bennings for their support during a time when she needed someone to lean on. It was gratifying to see the large congregation obviously devoted to Susan and Robert. She was looking forward to spring and attending as a new member.

Upon leaving the church, they went to lunch and afterward, made a short stop by the house to change clothes. Ryan wanted to rest so the others left him behind.

Neal was surprised when he saw Will's boat. "This is your fishing boat? You didn't mention it was a houseboat."

"Well, I've had it so long, it sounds pretentious to say houseboat."

"It looks like a small yacht. Mom will be spoiled."

Being an avid fisherman, Will was a little disappointed when they had to leave early for Neal's flight.

Katie volunteered to take Neal to the airport. She explained, "It won't be as far out of my way to take him." It was really an opportunity for her to have him to herself. They hadn't been alone since the kiss they shared in the garden.

"That is fine with me," Neal agreed, while suppressing his delight.

With his suitcases packed, Neal said his good-byes to the family. He turned to Will and said, "I understand why my mother is so happy. You're a good man, and I know you'll cherish her. It's been a pleasure visiting with you." It was much different than the cool reception during his late arrival.

Will, touched by Neal's kind words, grasped him by the arm. "I'm glad you were able to come for the holiday; have a safe trip."

Katie was in the driver's seat waiting on Neal. Will walked to her door and demanded she say something to Ryan and Deborah before she departed. She slipped out of the car, stood beside the driver side door, and waved to them saying, "I enjoyed spending time with you." Seeing her father's shocked expression, she quickly jumped back into her automobile.

Will shook his head with disapproval but didn't want to acknowledge her continued impolite behavior. He would have to be satisfied that she volunteered to take Neal to the airport.

As they pulled down the driveway, Neal said, "So the airport wasn't out of your way?"

"I'm glad we'll have some time together before my flight. It seems as if our walk was weeks ago."

"Neal, I've wanted to know how you feel about me. This has all happened so fast."

"Well, I want our relationship to continue. I really have enjoyed being with you, although it has been brief. May I call you?"

"Yes, I'd like that very much."

As they neared the airport, Katie asked Neal if he would mind her waiting with him in the terminal. He gladly agreed. They stayed together until it was necessary for Neal to go through security. Katie couldn't help herself. She reached out to him, and he was eager to hold her in his arms. They embraced for what seemed to be an eternity, and then Neal pulled her back and kissed her. It was quite evident this was much more than either of them had imagined. Neal promised to return to Atlanta whenever he could, and Katie held back tears as he walked away.

$$\mathcal{f}$$

"Will, we've had a marvelous holiday. The time has passed too swiftly. It will be Christmas before we will see each other again."

"It will be here before you know it, though I feel the same way. One day, you won't have to leave."

"I like the thought of not leaving," Deborah said.

"God has brought such joy through our tragedies. Todd and Jamie are buying a home, and will be moving. I didn't think the idea would appeal to me, but the anticipation of another grandchild and their renewed commitment makes me so thankful for God's blessings. It will also be nice to have the house to ourselves."

"It is wonderful how things have worked out for Todd. He confided to me about wanting Jamie's forgiveness and to raise the boys in a Christian home. Todd has changed in the short time I have known him."

"Yes, he seems much more content."

"I want to thank you for agreeing to have my family visit. You have won my children over, and I'm grateful we could spend this time together."

"I feel a kinship to your children already. Seeing Ryan and the strides he has made in his recovery is a real miracle. I also enjoyed meeting Neal, Megan, and her family. It was an outstanding Thanksgiving."

Before leaving on Monday, Deborah had a request for Betsy. "Betsy, Will and I have decided to have the wedding catered, and you will be a guest; however, I want to ask a big favor of you. Would you make your special cake for our wedding cake?"

Betsy happily agreed. "Yes, it can be my gift to you."

Deborah and Ryan packed their bags, and Todd carried them to the car. Jamie kept the twins at home so Will and Deborah could enjoy their final moments together. The trip to the airport seemed shortened, even with the congested downtown Atlanta traffic. Soon Deborah and Ryan would be in the air and back in New Jersey. She was envious of Ryan's eagerness to return, though she understood how he felt. Donna would be waiting, and he tried not to allow his separation from her interfere with meeting his soon-to-be family in Georgia.

When they arrived at the airport, Will's leg was bothering him, and he knew he couldn't make the long walk through the terminal; he would have to stay in the parking lot. Balancing on his cane, he held Deborah tight with his other hand. "I love you, darling. I'll be coming north next month. You'll have to pray for a white Christmas. I haven't seen significant snow this far south since the snow-apocalypse crippled Atlanta. You can't consider the flakes we occasionally have to be real snow. It doesn't accumulate and it hardly ever falls at Christmastime."

Deborah shook her head to let Will know she concurred. She couldn't seem to speak. Deborah knew if she started to talk it would trigger the tears filling her eyes.

Todd helped carry the bags to the terminal and then shook Ryan's hand. He hugged Deborah and said, "Have a safe trip, Mom." Deborah's eyes couldn't contain the weight of her tears, and water droplets flowed down her cheeks. Todd had become like one of her children. They had established a great rapport in such a short period of time. Deborah's thoughts turned to Katie, and the desire she had for a relationship with her.

The flight home was a quiet one. Ryan had fallen asleep and Deborah struggled with the emptiness she felt having to leave Will behind. She comforted herself with thoughts of Christmas and snow on the ground.

Chapter Twenty-Six

Donna was waiting with expectancy at the airport terminal for Ryan's return. His face lit up when he saw her, and she ran to embrace him. Deborah was thrilled her son had found someone as sweet as Donna to love. *There are blessings that come through tragedy*, Deborah pondered.

They quickly made their way through the baggage area. The air was chilly as she walked outside, and Deborah knew she would enjoy the transition to weather in Atlanta. The temperature had been in the seventies the entire week of their late November visit.

A stack of mail was waiting for Deborah when she arrived home. Donna had been thoughtful and picked up the mail while she was out of town. She called Will to let him know she was home, and when she hung up, she felt miserable. Her solitary existence was no longer desirable; the idea of being alone was unbearable.

Deborah sat down at her desk to edit the pages written before Thanksgiving.

Sipping hot chocolate, seated in front of the roaring fire, Alan's wide-eyed gaze made it clear to everyone gathered in the room he was deeply in love with Beverly.

Maybe I should change it to everyone gathered at the lodge, she thought.

Deborah got lost in her work, and the sun set long before she finished. She realized she hadn't heard from Neal since his return home, so she called to see how he was feeling. She wanted to make certain his ride to the airport with Katie had gone well.

Neal was aloof and not very talkative. He made the excuse, "I had a rough day at work, and am extremely tired." Deborah wondered if pairing Neal with Katie during the family gathering was the reason for his moodiness.

The following days seemed to drag on. Deborah went through the motions of maintaining her routine, but the highlight of her day was the long conversation with Will each night.

One evening, Megan called and asked Deborah to Christmas shop with her. There was a dismal tone to her voice, so Deborah asked, "Megan, is there anything wrong?"

"Mom, I didn't want to tell you yet, but Jason may be downsized soon. His company is laying off all the workers in Jason's division. Ever since the new merger, Jason has been concerned it might happen. It really takes the joy out of the season when we aren't sure if we'll have money available for our Christmas purchases. I felt if you came with me, it would distract me from my worries."

"It's been lonely without Will, so I also need your company. We'll plan on spending tomorrow together. The Lord can change the situation if we pray for his direction."

The mall was filled with the noise of shoppers and festive music. It appeared to Deborah that everyone had caught the spirit of Jesus' birth, even if they didn't believe in the reason for the season. The two women strolled past decorated store windows. Once in a while, an item would catch their eye, and they would enter to make a purchase. They soon were weighed down with packages and decided it was time to leave.

"Megan, take High Street on the way home, I love seeing the decorations."

As they made a right turn onto High Street, they descended the hill to view its large colonial homes. Most were painted white with immense round pillars. The porches were decked with swags of pine garlands and large red velvet bows and candles in the windows emitted a soft glow. "I never get tired of seeing these homes at Christmas. They make me feel as though, for a few minutes, there is peace on earth."

"I know what you mean," Megan agreed.

"Will you and the girls be able to help me decorate my house this year? I want it to look perfect."

"Of course we will; they will be thrilled when I tell them."

Making preparations for Will's visit gave Deborah a renewed sense of purpose. During one of their nightly talks, Will said, "Katie called and wanted to know if you would mind her coming to New Jersey with me? Needless to say, I was shocked, but it would give her a chance to make amends for her previous behavior. I told her I would let her know."

Deborah answered, "Of course, I would love to have her visit." She was pleased to know it was Katie's idea and hoped Christmas would bring the families even closer together. During the conversation, Deborah spoke of her concern for Megan. "Will, Jason's company is downsizing, and he'll probably lose his job soon. Will you speak with him at

Christmas? Megan mentioned that he doesn't want to discuss it with anyone, but I thought he might talk to you."

"Yes, I would be glad to; it must be difficult for him."

Neal called the next day, and Deborah remarked, "Katie has decided to come with Will to Mount Holly."

"That's great, Mom, I'm glad we'll be spending more time together." His apparent pleasure surprised Deborah—unaware Neal and Katie had been e-mailing each day and spending hours on the phone each night.

Deborah expressed, "It would be nice if you could make her feel at home during the holidays."

"You can count on me, Mom. I have decided to take leave from work most of the week." Little did Deborah know, Neal had been applying to companies in the Atlanta area while Katie clandestinely searched for a house.

When December 20 came, Deborah couldn't wait to decorate. Her enthusiasm was contagious. Megan brought the girls over to trim the tree, and Neal and Jason were in charge of decorating the roof peaks with icicle lights. Deborah hung a poinsettia wreath on the door and placed a large wreath of lights over the garage. As they finished the decorations, snowflakes began to float down from the sky. Will was due to arrive in two days, and everything seemed complete.

Chapter Twenty-Seven

A light snow was falling, and traffic was extremely heavy as Deborah drove to the airport. She was late arriving and had to page Will. "I'm so relieved that you were only delayed," Will said as he pulled her close. Reserved with her greeting, she didn't kiss Will so Katie wouldn't feel uncomfortable.

"Did you have a pleasant flight?" Deborah asked Katie.

"It was much shorter than I thought; we had some turbulence, but otherwise it was fine." Then Katie did something unexpected; she extended outstretched arms toward Deborah.

Will was speechless.

Deborah reached for Katie, and they hugged. Deborah and Will were stunned by Katie's actions.

They made their way to Deborah's car with very little conversation. The trip to Mount Holly took much longer than normal. Snow was continuing to fall, and Katie enjoyed watching the flakes swirling outside the car window. It had been years since she had seen snow covering the ground. As they drove down High Street, Katie commented, "Look, Dad, the houses resemble the older section of Gainesville, Georgia. They have the same large round columns with wrap around porches."

Descending the hill where the buildings downtown narrowed, Will said, "This area reminds me of my childhood in Pennsylvania, where mother and I used to shop. The stores are small and connected to each other; the decorations and being covered in snow is exactly the way I remember them."

Deborah pulled into the driveway of her large, ranch-style home, decorated with its lights and wreaths. She noticed her youngest son's car parked on the street.

Neal had left work early, anticipating Katie's visit, and opened the door. "Neal, I didn't expect to see you until later tonight." His mother looked at him curiously when she spoke.

"They were having the Christmas party at work, and I didn't feel like hanging around that crazy crowd, so I escaped early."

"Good, you can keep Katie company."

It was hard for Katie to hide her excitement at seeing Neal again. They were cordial with their greetings, so their parents wouldn't suspect anything. Neal made plans for being alone with Katie, but it seemed they weren't going to materialize as Ryan joined them in the living room.

"Hi guys, Donna called and said she'll be here soon for dinner."

"Oh, I can't wait to meet her. I'm sorry she didn't join us for Thanksgiving," Katie commented.

Deborah showed Katie and Will to their bedrooms and then went to the kitchen to finish preparing dinner. Ryan had been left in charge of watching the sirloin roast Deborah put in the oven before going to the airport, and he had the potatoes peeled and cut. There was just the salad to fix and the other vegetables to steam. She purchased a New York-style cheesecake for dessert so Deborah was confident her first meal prepared for Will would be delicious.

The doorbell rang, and Neal went to answer it. "Hi, Donna, come on in; dinner's almost ready. You haven't met Katie yet." Neal walked to the living room where Katie and Ryan were waiting. "Donna, this is Katie." Donna extended her hand as Katie stood.

"Donna, it's so nice to finally meet you. Ryan told me all about you at Thanksgiving; he really missed you."

Donna sat next to Katie, and the two of them chatted about everything. They almost ignored the two men sitting on the opposite sides of them until Deborah announced, "While I do the dishes, you young people can talk in the other room; Will is going to help me in the kitchen."

Later in the evening, Megan arrived with the girls to also welcome Will. Jason called and said he would be late; he wasn't ready to share the bad news of receiving his final paycheck. He needed time to himself after losing his job. The pink slip in his topcoat pocket was crumpled from the frustration he felt over the company's insensitivity to release their employees before the end of the year. When he finally arrived, he tried to be lighthearted with his greeting, but Will sensed his uneasiness.

When the family was gathered in the living room, Ryan surprised everyone by pulling a ring from his pocket. There was no doubt to anyone in the room that Donna's answer would be yes.

Ryan put the ring on her finger, and Donna took his face in her hands and kissed him. She then said, "Yes, now it's official." Their joy was contagious, and no one noticed the wink Neal gave Katie. She smiled and winked back.

While the family was congratulating the newly engaged couple, Will took the opportunity to take Jason aside to speak with him. "Jason, I noticed something seemed to be bothering you when you arrived. Have you received bad news?"

"Yes, I don't know how I'm going to tell Megan about receiving my final paycheck. I can't believe how heartless our company could be to ruin our Christmas."

"Deborah mentioned the situation was inevitable, so I hope you don't mind if I make a pitch for my company. I could really use another manager for my third store, and I understand your degree is in accounting. Home improvement may seem out of your element, but the employees at the Woodstock store know how to run the day-to-day operation. I just want someone to oversee the employees, and if you could handle the payroll and accounting, it would help us immensely. My accountant, Rob, is retired. When my wife died, he offered to step in and help with Sherry's responsibilities, but Rob would like to travel and enjoy his retirement. He asked me last week if I could find someone to replace him. I can't offer the amount you were making, but taxes and housing are much more affordable in Atlanta. It would make Deborah happy as well."

"I wasn't expecting this; I'll have to think about it."

"Take your time, but there will be a place for you if you want it."

"Thank you, Will. It does help to know how much you care."

"This is not an act of sympathy. My son has been losing his family due to the responsibility of managing all three stores. I've promised him we would bring in additional management to ease his workload. Someone of your experience and caliber would be an asset for us."

"It does ease my mind knowing I have an answer to this dilemma. Taking care of my family has always been my number one priority, and you know Megan would be thrilled by the idea of living near her mother. She's never been more than thirty minutes away from her. Give me time to think about your offer."

"You can have all the time you need."

Chapter Twenty-Eight

The next morning Deborah went to the kitchen to brew the coffee. Katie was already sitting at the table with a glass of juice. She had purposely risen early to have time alone with Deborah. She wanted the opportunity to ask for Deborah's forgiveness. "I hope you don't mind me helping myself to some juice."

"No, I'm glad you're making yourself at home."

"Deborah, I think I should apologize for my terrible behavior. I really haven't been very kind. I want you to know I'm glad you have given my father such happiness. He was a different person after Mother died. He seems to be himself recently, and I know you're the one responsible for the change. Will you please forgive me?"

"Oh Katie, strange circumstances got us off on the wrong foot. It's important to me that we be friends. I love your father, and I pray we can be a real family." Deborah reached her arms out as she had done in Atlanta. This time, Katie hurried over and embraced her. Will walked in to see the two women he loved together at last. He didn't want to spoil the moment, so he went into the living room. After several minutes, he entered the kitchen asking, "Where's my breakfast?"

"If you're going to be demanding, I'll just have to send you back to Atlanta," teased Deborah.

Will put his arm around her, and whispered quietly in her ear. "It seems there's been a breakthrough." Deborah just smiled at him then kissed him on the cheek.

"Breakfast will be served soon. I'm the only cook in this house."

"Maybe we should have asked Betsy to come," Katie said.

"I'm sure she's enjoying her family since Todd took Jamie to Colorado to spend a few days with her parents. We could never get Betsy to leave before," said Will. He turned to Katie and asked, "How do you like having a white Christmas?"

"It's a little strange, but I really think it might be my most favorite Christmas ever." Will had hoped for a change in Katie, but her transformation was a miracle.

After breakfast Deborah asked, "Katie, I need to go to the mall later, would you like to join me? Your father can keep Ryan company."

"I would love to. What woman doesn't like to shop?"

Deborah was excited. This would help to strengthen the tie just created between them. She put the breakfast dishes in the dishwasher, and made a list of items she would need to purchase. Katie had gone to her room to change clothes. It was then that Neal pulled into the driveway, hoping to take Katie for a ride.

Deborah met him at the door. "Neal, you're here early. You and Ryan can keep Will busy while Katie and I go to the mall." A look of disappointment came to Neal's face. "Don't be sad faced. Will said there are football games on today. It will be great for you men to enjoy the day together." Katie bounced down the hallway, announcing she was ready. She hadn't noticed Neal, as he was standing in the doorway out of view. He walked out, so she could see him.

"Neal, when did you arrive?"

"I just got here."

Deborah was busy preparing for her outing and was ignoring the conversation between them. She left to get her purse from the bedroom.

"I thought we would spend the afternoon together. My mother informed me you'll be with her."

"I'm sorry. I agreed so I could get to know her a little better. We were able to discuss our differences this morning, which helped ease the tension between us."

"I guess it's important you have this time. But don't plan anything for tomorrow. I'll make an excuse so we can finally have time for ourselves. I've had less time to talk to you here than when you're in Atlanta."

"Spending time with you is a priority for me, although we're not ready to announce our feelings to the family yet." Katie looked around then kissed Neal quickly on the cheek.

Deborah appeared, and the two women left for an afternoon at the mall. They found several gifts for the men, then treated themselves to a frothy cappuccino at the Coffee Shop. Katie asked, "Do you mind if we stop at the Coach store?"

"That's a great idea. I forgot about the wallet I wanted to buy for Donna; I can get one there."

Katie inquired, "Do you have a Dillard's?"

"I've never been to Dillard's, but we have a Macy's."

"I want to buy a sweater; I must admit I didn't really prepare for the cold weather."

As they were leaving, Katie said, "Deborah, I've really had fun today. Being a little bit of a rebel, I refused shopping trips with my mother."

"When I get to Atlanta, you must take me to Dillard's and some of your favorite places. It will be helpful to have a woman who knows her way around the malls."

"Deborah, I would really like to take you shopping. There are some unique outlets, and I need to take you to Alpine Bakery not far from Dad's house. Everything they make is delicious."

"You're making me hungry. How do you feel about going out for dinner?"

"That's a great idea. We'll just have to persuade the guys."

Deborah pulled into the driveway. "When it comes to food, they don't need to be convinced."

The men were engrossed in a football game when the women arrived home. The noise of cheering for a just-scored touchdown was the first sound Deborah heard as she entered the foyer. She went to the family room, and Katie followed.

Will was pleased to see them. "Back so soon?"

Deborah quipped, "It's later than you think. I've decided we should go out to dinner tonight. How would you like prime rib?"

"Sounds good to me," said Katie.

"If you're going to Charlie's Other Brother, count me in, and it's Donna's favorite too," answered Ryan. They all agreed Charlie's was a great choice, and Ryan called Donna to meet them at the restaurant by seven o'clock.

The hostess escorted them to a large table where they paired off: Will with Deborah, Donna with Ryan, and Neal next to

Katie. Neal reached over and squeezed Katie's hand under the table. "Neal, stop." Katie whispered. She was afraid someone would notice his fond gesture.

Deborah looked over to see Katie frowning at Neal. She had made such progress with Katie during the shopping trip, now she felt responsible for Katie being uncomfortable with the seating arrangements. Will sensed her frustration. "What's wrong dear?"

"Katie looks annoyed sitting next to Neal."

"Nonsense, it's only dinner; she'll be fine."

Deborah wasn't sure, but she tried to put the incident behind her and enjoy the rest of the evening.

Katie commented, "This is really a quaint place with its unique movie posters. The fireplace looks lovely decorated in lights, and the large pine wreath is beautiful. It feels so homey."

"The prime rib is really juicy; I'm glad you chose this place," Will said.

Deborah reminded everyone of the Christmas festivities for the following night. "We always open our presents on Christmas Eve and allow the children to stay up late to play with their gifts. The neighbors arrive for a buffet at eight o'clock and then we attend a midnight church service. You should all sleep late, to be rested for the long night ahead."

Deborah's Christmas traditions were different from Will's childhood and the years spent with Sherry. They would open their gifts on Christmas morning, and yet Will and Katie were looking forward to Deborah's celebration.

They left the restaurant, and Katie got into the backseat with Neal. Deborah noticed they were sitting close together.

She dismissed the thought as she recalled the look of what she thought was an annoyed Katie at dinner.

Neal whispered in Katie's ear, "I want to take you out for breakfast tomorrow, so we can have some time alone."

"Okay, but not too early," Katie reluctantly agreed. She had promised Deborah she would help with the preparations for the next evening, so Neal's invitation didn't have the appeal it should have.

As they parked in the driveway, Neal held the door for Katie and said good night to everyone. He got into his car and sped away. Katie quickly said good night and went to her room. Breakfast at eight o'clock would be earlier than she hoped, yet she beamed with the anticipation of finally spending time with Neal.

Will and Deborah sat up talking, and the hours flew by as they found such pleasure in each other's company. It was precious time together, and they didn't have to worry about the lateness of the hour. It was good training for Christmas Eve.

Chapter Twenty-Nine

The alarm clock beeped, and Katie jumped out of bed. It took her a little longer getting dressed, as she was trying not to make any noise. She looked out of the window and could see Neal pulling into the driveway, so she gave him a quick wave. With the cold December air, he waited in the car to keep the heat circulating.

Katie grabbed her coat and gloves and quietly walked through the hallway. No one was stirring as she opened the door and ran toward Neal's car.

Neal waited until they drove away from the house and then pulled over to the curb. There had been phone conversations and e-mails, but with many miles between them, they had longed for this moment. He reached for Katie's neck and brought her face toward him for their first kiss since Thanksgiving.

"Katie, I've grown to love you in such a short time. Will you marry me?"

"Neal, this is a little unexpected, but I know we belong together. Yes, I'll marry you."

"Do you want a big church wedding?"

"No, I really prefer to elope."

"That was going to be my suggestion. I just got a job offer in Atlanta, the start date is January 15, and my realtor said he has a buyer for my house."

"How wonderful. I found the perfect house for you, I mean us, just blocks from Jamie and Todd. It's vacant and available immediately. All of the pieces are coming together perfectly."

"Do you think our parents will understand?"

"Maybe we should wait to tell them."

"Won't your dad know if you move in with me after we're married?"

"He never visits me, so he won't know unless I tell him."

"Are you free for New Year's Eve? We can be married and start the year in Atlanta."

"This is all too incredible. We just met last month. Do you think our parents will be shocked?"

"If they did hear, I'm sure it might upset them during this time. How can we keep them from finding out about our plans? " Neal was having doubts they could hide being married, especially from his mother.

"They'll be busy. I think we can pull it off."

"New Year's Eve is only a week away, but I don't want to wait any longer. I'm anxious to start my life with you, Katie. I hope you feel the same."

"All I really want is to be with you." Neal wrapped his arms around her and caressed her lips. Katie held him close and responded with passion.

Neal was pleased with her answer, and his face reflected the happiness he felt. "Now, I promised you breakfast."

ℐ

It was after nine in the morning when Deborah awoke. Ryan and Will weren't up, and she thought Katie was still in her room. As she put the coffee on, Ryan joined his mother in the kitchen. He was excited about spending his first Christmas with Donna. Deborah hadn't spent much quality time with Ryan since his engagement. The morning gave them time to discuss the plans taking shape in both of their lives. It was the special mother-and-son conversation she had missed in recent years.

"Mom, I've got some amazing news for you. I'm planning to go to Bible College. Since my accident, the Lord has been speaking to me about dedicating my life to the ministry. I hadn't felt I could share this with you until now. Donna has always felt a need to work in the mission field. She desires to use her training to help others. We're not sure where God will take us, but we both want God's will in our lives. I will be enrolling for the spring semester."

"Ryan, what marvelous news! I can't be happier for you and Donna. When you were lying in your hospital bed so lifeless, I prayed God would not only spare your life but give you a deeper walk with him."

"I'm really glad you'll have Will to take care of you. You may not have been supportive of our possibly going overseas if your life hadn't gone in a different direction as well."

"Nonsense, I have always supported whatever you chose to do. How could I have asked for a greater plan for your life? You know how much I love Donna; she's like one of my own children. It's comforting to know she'll be at your side. It's hard to find true love, and a partner who shares your devotion to the Lord. Love and compatibility are important in a marriage. If I hadn't found Will, I probably wouldn't have married again."

It was almost noon when Will finally joined them in the kitchen.

"Good morning, sleepyhead. You know it's almost after noon," Deborah teased.

"You gave me instructions to sleep late. After you kept me up half the night talking, I followed your mandate. Where's Katie? Hasn't she shown up yet?"

"No, does she usually sleep late?"

"She was always an early riser when she lived at home."

Just then the front door opened, and Neal and Katie made their way to the kitchen.

"We were wondering about you," said Will.

"Neal offered to buy me breakfast and show me the area this morning. I hope you weren't worried."

"No, your father just got up. We thought you might be sleeping late, too."

"I can't sleep late, even when I'm ordered to. I've always been a morning person. That's why I took Neal up on his invitation. We stopped to see a Christmas display on the way back. It was beautiful but extremely cold outside. I'm not accustomed to this weather, so we decided to come back for hot coffee."

"I just brewed a new pot for your father. I'll get some cups." Deborah took Neal aside and thanked him for taking Katie to breakfast. She was glad he took her suggestion of making her feel welcomed.

There was much to do before the rest of the family joined them. Katie assisted Deborah with preparations for the big buffet. There were presents still to wrap, so they all retreated to their rooms at various times to place the paper and special bows on the gifts that would adorn the bottom of the tree.

Megan, Jason, and their daughters arrived late in the afternoon. Seeing the tree surrounded by so many packages, the girls were eager to open their presents. They went on a hunt for those marked with their names. Deborah distracted her granddaughters by asking for help placing candies on the gingerbread house she baked earlier in the week.

Megan gave Will a big hug and whispered a thank you for his offer to Jason. Planting a kiss on the top of her head, Will said, "I hope he takes my proposal seriously, it would be a blessing to have you living near us in Atlanta."

"Hey, what's this? You two are being awfully chummy," declared Deborah.

"Oh, it's just our little secret," said Will.

Everyone waited for Donna to arrive. When the girls heard her car, they ran to the front door and quickly ushered her to the living room. Donna took her seat next to Ryan. Deborah knew her granddaughters could wait no longer. Shrieks of excitement would come from each one as they tore through the boxes. When they were finished, Deborah handed the adults their gifts.

Will gave Deborah an opulent gold watch, and she bought him a fishing rod—one Todd said he had been eyeing for months. Will was ecstatic. It was just what he wanted, although, he would have to have Deborah bring it with her when she drove south in the spring.

Neal stood and cleared his throat. "May I have your attention?" Everyone stopped what they were doing and turned toward him. "I have some fantastic news. I will be transferring to Atlanta in January." Astonished by his announcement, it took a moment before the family rushed to him to give him their blessings.

Deborah was thrilled with his news. It meant he would be living close to her after she married.

It was then Jason stood and said, "I also have an announcement. Some of you don't know I was downsized and lost my job." All eyes got big and stared directly at him. "However, I've had another proposal I couldn't refuse, and since everyone seems to be leaving New Jersey, we thought it was time for us to also make a move. Megan and I have decided to accept an offer from Will for a position in his Woodstock store." The family was dazed by the news. After a few seconds, they all congratulated him. Megan grabbed her mother by the neck and started to weep. "We'll all be together in Atlanta, and we won't have to travel the terribly long distance to see one another."

Deborah got everyone's attention and said, "Are there any more announcements we should know about?" Neal gave Katie a quick wink, and she smiled with delight, contemplating their secret New Year's celebration.

With the help of Megan, Donna, and Katie, Deborah started to place the food on the table. It wasn't long before the guests began arriving for the annual buffet. Sounds of laughter and music filled the house as Donna sat at the piano and led everyone in Christmas carols. When the last neighbor left, the family prepared to leave for church.

Each year the children would participate in a performance of the Nativity. Deborah's oldest granddaughter Sara was cast as the angel who watched over the Christ child lying in the manger. The other girls sang with the youth choir, leading the congregation in hymns of the season. It was always a service Deborah enjoyed.

After returning from service, Megan's daughters fell asleep in the den. Jason and Neal had to carry them to the car. The children's presents were stacked under the Christmas tree. They would be returning the next day for Christmas dinner and could play with them then. Kathy, the youngest, wouldn't release the stuffed bear bought by Uncle Ryan, so it went home with her.

Donna and Ryan went to the foyer to say good night, while Neal told Katie to meet him in the den.

Neal peeked out of the door to make sure no one would be entering the room. He pulled a box from his pocket. "Katie, I was hoping you would say yes, so I bought this last week."

As Katie opened the box, her eyes widened. Inside was a diamond ring. "Neal, I can't wear this yet. Not if it's going to be a secret."

"You can wear it when you're with me until we tell our parents."

Katie put her arms around Neal's neck and kissed him. "Neal, I love you."

At that moment, Ryan walked past the door to the den. He pushed the door open and saw Katie and Neal embracing. Ryan gave Katie a wink and said, "What's going on?"

"How long have you been there? What did you hear?" asked Neal.

"Long enough. Mom thinks you two are having trouble getting along. I see it's just the opposite."

"Ryan, we have tried to keep our feelings confidential. Mother and Will might not understand our short courtship."

"What's really going on?"

"I suppose we can trust you, but please keep it to yourself. Katie and I are eloping next week. We plan to be married New Year's Eve."

"What! How do you think you can keep that from Mom?"

"She'll be busy with her wedding plans and getting the house ready to sell, so she shouldn't suspect anything. I'll have the new job in Atlanta, and Katie has found me, I should say us, a house."

"You really have been plotting this move."

"Yes, now promise you'll keep this to yourself. Don't even tell Donna."

"I'll try, brother. It's really sudden, but I wish you both the best."

"Thank you, Ryan," said Katie.

"I'm not sure I like the fact you'll be beating me to the altar."

Will and Deborah came walking down the hallway. "Where is everybody?"

"We're in here, Mom," said Ryan.

They joined the boys and Katie, and the conversation changed to the Christmas Eve celebration.

"This was very different, but I really enjoyed the way you spend your Christmas," said Katie.

"It's not over yet. There's the big turkey dinner tomorrow," said Ryan.

Deborah stated, "Speaking of turkey dinner, I'd better go to bed so I'll be rested to prepare for our feast."

Chapter Thirty

C hristmas morning activities began early. There were pies to bake and the stuffing to make. With the pumpkin pies removed from the oven, Deborah concentrated on preparing the turkey.

Deborah watched the snow falling outside her kitchen window. It was covering the trees and made everything look so pristine. Will had wanted a white Christmas, and the Lord was giving him his desire, although Deborah hoped the snow wouldn't hinder the rest of the family from coming for dinner.

Katie was the first to join Deborah, and she beamed at the sight of the falling snow. "It's so pretty. Georgia has fantastic weather, but we miss out by not having a real winter season. Everything looks so clean, and the trees look like someone dusted them with silvery glitter."

A voice behind her said, "I knew you'd like the North for the holidays."

"Daddy, isn't it just the prettiest sight?"

"Yes, it is now, but I had to shovel it for years, and I don't think I have the same appreciation for it that you have."

"You loved winter when we were younger. We had so much fun flying down the hill behind your house on our sleds," Deborah reminded him.

"Deborah, do you still have a sled? I've never had the chance to sled ride," giggled Katie.

"I'm sure we have one or two in the garage. I've kept them for my granddaughters when they visit. Neal can take you out when he comes over. He called and said he'd join us for breakfast."

"Great, I can't wait." The excitement Katie displayed at the mention of Neal joining them for breakfast was construed to be over the sled riding, but her genuine feelings of spending time with him was the reason for her exuberance. She excused herself to fix her hair and dress before Neal arrived.

"You had me fooled in Montana with your John Wayne image, what happened to the young-at-heart fellow I met there?"

"Being reminded of our younger years, I suppose I wanted to impress you. The gray hair signifies more than wisdom. The accident made me feel my age."

"I'll get you back in shape in no time. Do you remember how we roller skated every week at the Ardmore Rink in Forest Hills?"

"Now that was a long time ago. I looked forward to Fridays during couples skate. I think I was about twelve the first time I asked you to skate with me."

The front door opened, and Neal yelled, "Anyone home?"

"We're in the kitchen, Neal. I need your help entertaining Will while I get the food prepared."

Neal was hoping to see Katie, but she was still primping and hadn't heard him arrive.

"Good morning, where's Katie? I thought she would be up by now."

"She is; she went to finish dressing and should be down soon," Deborah assured him.

"It looks like we may get several inches of snow today. The roads are covered, and I didn't see any trucks plowing."

"Those poor men have to get out on Christmas morning to clean the roads while we get to enjoy the snow. By the way, Katie wants to sled ride, and I said you would take her."

"Sure, sledding sounds like fun."

The dining room table was set and the coffee brewed as everyone gathered for breakfast. Deborah warmed some of the ham from the night before and scrambled a dozen eggs. There were also pastry leftovers, which she plated and carried to the table. It was a relief to Deborah to have the hostility Katie felt behind them. It was also evident Neal and Katie had become friends.

Like small children, the young couple spent the rest of the morning playing in the snow. There was a snowball fight as well as sliding down the hill cuddling together on the small wooden sled. Deborah watched them from the window and was thrilled to see the fun they were having. *Just like real brothers and sisters would do,* she thought. They came into the house covered in snow and craving hot coffee.

It was early afternoon when Megan arrived with her three daughters. Each one was anxious to tell their grandmother about all the new presents they received from Santa. "Wow, you must have been good this year," said Deborah.

Valerie asked, "Grandma, where did you put the presents we opened last night?" Deborah said their gifts were under the

Christmas tree, and they all ran down the hallway to the living room anxious to play with the toys.

For Deborah, preparing the Christmas dinner was particularly special. Betsy would probably be cooking the holiday dinners when she moved to Atlanta. To have Will and Katie united with her own family was heartwarming. It was just the beginning of many joy filled celebrations.

After enjoying the feast, Megan's family left, and Neal stole Katie away to make some final arrangements to meet for New Year's Eve.

They were in the den when Ryan and Donna walked in. Ryan asked, "May we join you? What's new with you two?"

"Of course, not much," was Neal's hasty reply.

Donna looked at Ryan and grinned. *What a strange answer,* she thought. Ryan just smiled back at her and gave a wink toward Katie.

Neal got a scowl on his face. "You've told Donna, haven't you?"

"Told me what?" Donna was surprised by Neal's reaction, and it spurred her curiosity.

"No, she doesn't know a thing." Ryan knew the cat was out of the bag, but there was nothing he could do about it.

"What's so secret you can't tell me?" Donna looked at Ryan and said, "I didn't think we had any secrets from each another."

Ryan peered at his brother. "You've done it to me now. Donna's not going to trust me anymore."

Neal's face was beet red. He knew he would have to share their clandestine engagement with Donna. Thoughts of how he was going to keep the news from his mother when he couldn't keep the information from his brother's fiancée were plaguing him. Katie sat silently listening as their elopement was revealed to Donna, nervous of her father's reactions should he overhear.

Katie had scheduled a flight home for the following day, using the excuse of needing to get back to work. She had other arrangements to make and packing to be done for meeting Neal later in the week. Their parents were not expecting what the New Year would bring.

Chapter Thirty-One

With Will back in Atlanta, Deborah spent her days shopping for invitations, coordinating dress fittings for the wedding party, and purchasing her dress. A trip with Megan to Neiman Marcus in Philadelphia yielded the most stunning tea-length, powder blue chiffon. She decided she would wear her hair down and chose a matching picture hat.

A few days later, Neal made a trip to New Jersey to settle on his house and was there while the movers packed his belongings. Deborah, sad about Neal leaving, consoled herself with the fact he would be living in Atlanta. She was able to spend a few days with him before he moved south. Neal wanted to share his marriage with his mother, but he had promised Katie they wouldn't tell their parents until they were sure Will and Deborah would understand.

Everything was falling into place with Megan and Neal planning to live in Atlanta and Ryan studying for the ministry. Deborah even found time for her writing and was excited to have completed her novel. She hadn't been sure how she was going to meet her deadline after Will's accident, but the days spent in the hospital with Ryan gave the extra time needed. She was ready to send the final manuscript changes to her editor. There was a great sense of satisfaction and relief now she could spend more time concentrating on her move.

By March, wedding preparations were well underway. Deborah called Katie about flying to New Jersey for a final fitting on her dress. Katie mentioned to Deborah she wasn't feeling well and thought she may have contracted the flu. She told Deborah she made an appointment to see her physician, and would notify Deborah when she would be arriving.

Katie enjoyed seeing Dr. Johnson. He had been a friend of her parents since she was a little girl. The doctor decided to take blood and urine samples because her symptoms were a little suspect. He said, "Katherine, I should have the results later."

That afternoon, Dr. Johnson called, "Katie, you're pregnant. Congratulations!"

Neal heard the phone ring and saw the shocked look on Katie's face. "What's wrong?"

"Nothing. I'm pregnant." She thanked the doctor and ended the call.

Neal ran to his wife and held her tight, "We're going to have to tell Mom and Dad right away."

"Why don't we wait until next week when your mother is in town?"

"That might work out better; we can tell them together."

Katie thought about her dress for the wedding and knew it wouldn't fit in two months. She felt she needed to contact Deborah immediately.

"Hello, Deborah."

"Katie, is it you?"

"Yes, I'm calling to let you know I can't be in the wedding party. I won't be coming to New Jersey for the fitting."

"Katie, is there a problem?"

"No, I just can't discuss it now. We can talk about it next week when you're in Atlanta."

Deborah was stunned. She couldn't imagine why Katie had changed her mind. "Thank you for letting me know." Confused, Deborah decided to phone Will. "Will, what's wrong with Katie? She just called and said she can't be in the wedding and didn't give me a reason for backing out. I thought we were on good terms."

"I have no idea. I'll stop by her apartment tomorrow after I see Dr. Johnson. I've been suffering with a cold and need some medicine."

"Katie mentioned she hadn't been feeling well and was going to see the doctor. Please call me when you know anything. I'm concerned about her."

Will sat in the examining room waiting for the doctor. As he came through the door, he greeted Will with, "Hello, Grandpa. Congratulations! You must be excited about your two new grandchildren on the way."

Will was astonished. "What! Is Jamie having twins again?"

"No, hasn't Katie told you?"

The news stunned him. "Katie?"

"Yes, I just gave her the good news yesterday."

Will was flabbergasted. Katie was pregnant. *How had it happened*? He didn't know she was even dating anyone. *Who was the father of the baby?* Will realized he hadn't been close to his daughter in the past few months. Except for seeing her at church, he hadn't spent any real time with her since Christmas.

When Will left the doctor's office, he went straight to Katie's apartment. A strange woman answered the door and informed

Will she had lived there since the beginning of February, but she thought the name of the girl who moved was Katherine. Will was shocked. The idea Katie would move without telling him was unthinkable. But then again, she was keeping the baby a secret. *Where was Katie living?* He picked up his cell phone and called Katie's number, but he got a recording. He didn't want to leave a message because he wanted to speak directly to his daughter.

Will tried to think of a way to locate her and decided to see if Jamie knew anything. He drove to Roswell without calling so he wouldn't alarm her. Will tried to act as normal as possible. He wanted to question Jamie without making her suspicious.

"Dad, I spoke to Katie yesterday, and she was in a great mood. She didn't mention that she moved. Have you called her office or spoken to Neal?"

"Thank you for your ideas. I'll go by Neal's house on the way home."

As he pulled into Neal's driveway, he noticed the garage door open and Katie's car parked inside. Will rang the doorbell and Katie answered.

"Katie, I've been looking all over for you. What are you doing here? Why didn't you tell me you moved? Where are you living now?"

"I live here."

"What do you mean you live here? Are you living with Neal?"

"Yes, I am Dad."

"How long has this been going on?"

"Since Neal moved down in January."

Will was livid. He stalked away from the door and got into his car. Katie ran after him yelling, "Dad, wait."

Will was upset with his daughter and Neal. *How will I tell Deborah?* It involved her son, but Will knew he didn't want to deal with the situation by himself.

Will pulled his phone from his pants pocket and called Deborah. "Hello, Deborah. I need to discuss something with you."

"Will, you sound upset. What's happened?"

"Katie is pregnant. She has been living with Neal since January."

"What?"

"You heard me. I think Neal's the father."

"Will, are you sure?"

"Yes, Katie told me she was living with Neal. I need you to come down to speak with your son." Will didn't mean to be cold. His daughter had been rebellious in the past; however, this was totally unexpected.

"I'll leave tomorrow."

Ryan overheard the conversation and suspected his brother's secret was about to be revealed.

Deborah saw Ryan in the hallway and said, "It's urgent for me to be in Atlanta tomorrow."

"Is everything all right?"

"I'll tell you about it after I arrive."

Ryan went to his room and called Neal. "Hey, brother, what's going on in Atlanta?"

"What do you mean, why are you calling?"

"Mom will be down there tomorrow at Will's request."

"Great, now maybe we can explain we're married. Will came by and found out Katie was living here. He freaked and left without giving Katie a chance to explain. He hasn't been taking her phone calls either."

"No wonder Mom seemed to be concerned. I told you it would be hard to keep your marriage a secret."

"I do have some good news to tell you. Katie is pregnant."

"Congratulations. You not only beat me to the altar, but you will be a dad first. I always believed I would have kids before you. Give my love to Katie, and I'll talk to you soon."

The next day, Deborah arrived at Hartsfield-Jackson Airport and looked around the terminal for Will. She noticed him limping toward her. He had a frown on his face and she took a deep breath before greeting him. "Hello, how are you doing?"

"I feel as well as to be expected, under the circumstances. This situation has been revolting."

Will was being very distant. Deborah knew she shouldn't say very much until they were alone. Secure inside the car, she remarked, "Will, maybe you have misjudged the situation. You may not know all of the facts."

He answered in a harsh tone, "Dr. Johnson said Katie is pregnant. Katie said she was living with Neal. What else can I conclude from those facts?"

"Let's give them a chance to explain what happened. You said Katie has been faithful to church and living for God."

"In her condition, she can't be. It must have been for show. When I think how she and your son have been deceiving us, it makes my blood boil."

Deborah didn't say anything more. The tension in the car was insufferable. She and Will were having their first argument, and she didn't want it to continue.

When they got to Neal's house, Deborah rang the doorbell. Neal opened the door and invited them inside. Without saying a word, Deborah hugged both Neal and Katie and sat down on the couch. Choosing to sit in the recliner several feet away, Will made it clear to everyone in the room he didn't want to be near Deborah. Katie and Neal looked at each other and grimaced. Neal wondered if their marriage was the sole factor for Will's anger. He never wanted to create problems for his mother and Will.

Deborah began the conversation. "I think you know why I'm here. Will said you are living together and Katie is pregnant. Is that true?"

"Yes, but I didn't tell Daddy I was pregnant."

"No, Dr. Johnson told me. I didn't even hear it from my own daughter. Of course I'm not surprised you weren't proud of it."

"Will, please calm down and let them explain."

"Mom, Katie and I eloped in December. We were married New Year's Eve. We didn't think you would understand, so we kept it a secret. We knew the moment we met that we were to be together. We felt it would complicate things if we told you. When we got the news about the baby, we agreed we needed to tell you during your next trip. I know now it was wrong to keep you in the dark. We didn't just move in together. Will didn't let us explain the facts. We love each other, and we're excited about the baby and hoped you would be too."

"This is wonderful."

"What's wonderful? Our children didn't have the courtesy to tell us they were getting married, and I had to find out my daughter moved and is having a baby from others. After all, Katie only met Neal at Thanksgiving. How could they have fallen in love?"

"I assure you, I have found the love of my life. I plan to take care of her and our child. It was sudden, but I knew the first time I saw her she was the woman I wanted to spend the rest of my life with. We didn't want a big wedding, and we didn't want to wait."

Deborah stated, "Do you understand what God has done?"

"Why are you blaming God? What does He have to do with this?"

"We won't have children of our own, but God is giving us a grandchild."

"What are you talking about? We have grandchildren."

"No, Will, this grandchild is special. It will belong to both of us. It will be blood related to both families."

Will got up and walked out of the door. He retrieved Deborah's bags from the car and returned to the house. As Neal held the door open, Will handed him the bags and walked back toward the car.

Deborah watched in disbelief as he pulled out of the driveway.

Katie burst into tears. "Deborah, I'm so sorry. I wanted to sabotage your relationship with my dad in the beginning. Now I've really done it. Please try to forgive me."

"Dear, it's not your fault. Your father needs time to consider what's happened."

"Mom, we were going to tell you next week. We didn't know Will would hear the news from the doctor."

"Everything will be fine. I'm elated about the baby." Deborah knew there was something else bothering Will. She didn't want the children to feel her concern. She thought Will should be satisfied with the good news. His daughter was married and he should have been thrilled about the baby.

Deborah asked Neal where they planned for her to sleep. He showed her to the guest room and brought her bags from the living room. Deborah needed to speak with someone who could keep the situation confidential, so she called Susan and made arrangements to have lunch with her the next day. She hoped Susan would have an idea for reaching Will during this time.

The following day, Deborah told Neal she needed to borrow his car to see Mrs. Benning. Susan was waiting for her at a nearby Italian restaurant. As Deborah shared the recent news, Susan was amazed. "How did Katie think she could keep her relationship with Neal such a secret? I'm really stunned by Will's reaction. It's puzzling he isn't delighted about the baby."

"Please help me to pray that Robert's sermon may help Will comprehend the situation with Neal and Katie."

Deborah felt a sense of relief after speaking with Susan and knew Will would understand if the Lord dealt with his heart. She was glad to have Susan as a friend and could count on her to pray for God's answer.

Will didn't contact Deborah all day Saturday.

Sunday morning brought the family together at church. Todd and his family sat with Deborah, Neal, and Katie. Will was nowhere in sight. Robert stood at the pulpit and began his message. He spoke of God's love and forgiveness. Deborah knew the Lord had heard her prayer but wished Will were with them. Robert also spoke about the importance of family and loving each other unconditionally. Todd motioned for Deborah to look toward the back of the sanctuary. She was pleasantly surprised to see Will seated close to the door. Deborah whispered a prayer of thanks to the Lord.

When the service ended, Will quickly exited the church and wasn't in the vicinity when the rest of the family left. Deborah thought Will would be changed by the words Robert spoke, and she didn't want to give up hope for him to apologize for his outburst. Neal and Katie looked dejected as they walked toward the car.

It was a quiet lunch, as no one wanted to mention Will's absence. Deborah went to the guest room to pack for returning to New Jersey. There was a knock at the front door, and Neal got up from reading the paper to answer it. To his surprise, it was Will.

"May I come in?"

"Yes, of course."

"Please get Katie and your mother. I have something to say to all of you."

Neal called for his mother and Katie to come to the living room where Will was waiting. Deborah was surprised to see him, as she hadn't heard the knock at the door. Katie came quickly out of her room and smiled at the sight of her father standing in front of them.

"I want to ask your forgiveness for my actions. It came as such a shock to me, Katie, that you and Neal were married and expecting a baby. I wouldn't allow myself to believe you would be so secretive about your condition. I also want to apologize to you, Deborah, for ignoring your view of the situation. It wasn't until I had time to let the words of this morning's sermon sink in, that I knew why it bothered me. I never told you, Katie, about the promise I made to your mother. She wanted you to have the biggest wedding in Atlanta. We didn't have the money to spend for our wedding, so she wanted your wedding to be extra special. It was her dying wish."

"Oh Daddy, of course I forgive you. We never wanted to hurt you. We both fell in love instantly, and everything fell into place with Neal transferring and buying the house. Our marriage shouldn't bring division in the family. When you wouldn't take my calls, it hurt to think you thought so little of my convictions and me. Why didn't you tell me about your promise to Mother about my wedding?" Katie grabbed Will and threw her arms around him.

"I never thought you would elope."

"Daddy, I never wanted a big wedding. It wasn't something I dreamed about. When Neal and I discussed it, we both preferred to elope. Please try to understand, we had the wedding we both wanted."

"I'm happy for you, and I know you love each other. Neal, I wasn't very kind to you. I do want to be your dad and friend." Neal joined Katie and wrapped his arms around Will.

As they separated from the group hug. Will stared at Deborah. "I lost you once and I can't think of life without you. Please know I love you with all my heart. You have always had a way of seeing the best in everything."

Deborah stood facing Will. "That's why it's important to have all the facts from the people directly involved and not secondhand where they can become distorted. I was also wrong when I assumed Katie didn't want to be in the wedding. Now I understand completely. Neal, since I have one less bridesmaid, will you walk me down the aisle?"

"Mom, it would be my pleasure."

Will embraced his daughter and kissed her on the forehead. "You'll make a great mother, and I can see how much you love Neal." Will then said, "Neal, please forgive me. Thank you for loving my daughter."

Deborah put her hand on Will's back. He turned around and looked directly into her eyes. "I'm ashamed of the way I've been acting toward you. I blamed you and you didn't deserve it. I'm sorry. Can you ever forgive me?"

Deborah smiled and said, "Just don't do it again. There's still enough time to call off the wedding."

She reached her arms up to embrace him.

Will suggested calling Todd and Jamie to celebrate with them. Katie asked if they could go to the restaurant where she and Neal ate the first night they met. Everyone agreed it was the perfect choice.

Chapter Thirty-Two

The final week before the wedding came quickly. With her house sold and possessions packed and sent to Georgia, Deborah was ready to start her new life with the man she adored. Will said he would make room to store her belongings until after the wedding.

It was Monday morning when Deborah stacked the boxes she would need immediately into her SUV. Megan and Donna stopped to see Deborah before she left for her trip south. They would be flying down with the rest of the family Friday morning. Deborah took one last look around her empty home. A home once filled with joy, a place her children were raised, and which held memories of the years spent with her first husband Ryan. Reflecting on all it meant to her brought tears to her eyes. She could see Megan was also tearing up.

"You're not having second thoughts are you, Mother?"

"No dear, I am completely satisfied; Atlanta will be my home now. I can leave without regrets knowing I'll be with the man I love, but I have so many memories tied to this place."

"You will have a wonderful life, and we'll come to Atlanta to help you make new memories," said Donna.

"Now I must be going. I want to arrive at Nancy's before dark." Deborah hugged them both and said she would see them on Friday.

A planned stop in Virginia to stay with her sister Nancy would allow time to visit before the hectic wedding activities. Nancy and her husband Jim would be following Deborah the rest of the way to Atlanta.

As she drove south, Deborah could see the greenery and flowers of spring everywhere. She thought of how glorious the garden would look, and Will told her the magnolias were in full bloom. What a blessing to begin their lives when nature was full of life. Deborah was thankful to have this time alone to enjoy God's wondrous universe. It made her realize how blessed she was. God had given her a man who was devoted to his faith. Of all the men He could have sent her way, He sent Will, a man who once held a very special place in her heart. Deborah found herself thanking God in a loud praise as she drove down the interstate. It didn't matter who heard or saw her, she was ecstatic, happier than she had been for a very long time.

Deborah pulled into her sister's driveway and honked the horn. Nancy and Jim came out to help her with her bags. She handed Jim a large box containing Nancy's dress.

"It's good to see you, Deborah. Are you ready for the big week?" Jim was a man that Deborah admired, a real gentleman.

"Yes, I thought I would be nervous, but I have such peace knowing this is God's will. Plus, Will has dealt with the majority of the work. I've e-mailed him lists of things to check and order each day. He'll be glad when I finally arrive to help him with the last minute details. Jamie, Will's daughter-in-law, has been a tremendous help to him, but she's due in two weeks and needs this time to rest."

They enjoyed dinner together, then Jim retreated to his study while Nancy and Deborah cleaned the dishes. It felt like old times with the two of them giggling in the kitchen. Deborah was grateful to have such a loving sister.

Nancy tried her dress on and it fit perfectly. This made them both breathe a sigh of relief, as Nancy had gained a few pounds since her last fitting.

They spent the rest of the evening discussing the wedding. Nancy asked, "Where are you spending your honeymoon?"

Deborah explained, "Will is taking care of those arrangements; he wants to surprise me. I trust his choice; wherever he chooses will be special."

The next morning, Jim packed their car and Deborah put the overnight bag in her front seat. As they left, Deborah realized she would never have to leave Will again.

Chapter Thirty-Three

Will was rocking impatiently on the front porch waiting for Deborah's arrival. He had abandoned the use of his cane and was now able to walk the garden path to the arbor he had built. Deborah had wanted a simple arch between the two magnolias, but Will wanted the place where they would say their vows to be unforgettable. He spent the previous two months designing and building a work of art. The arch had ornate scrollwork of flowers and doves on each side and a shelf on top to hold a bed of white roses. He was anxious to see Deborah's reaction.

As she entered the long driveway, Deborah noticed how perfect the magnolia trees lining each side of the roadway appeared. She felt as though she was driving onto a movie lot or the roadway in a portrait. This would be home. She felt a little like a princess making her way to the castle to live happily ever after. It may have been a childish thought, although even at her age she liked the idea. As she got closer to the house, she spied Will rocking on the porch.

Will waited for the car to pull up to the house and stop, then jumped up to open Deborah's door. They held each other as if they would never let go. Deborah could sense Will's relief that the time had finally arrived and they would be together forever.

Nancy and Jim greeted Will. "What a magnificent home you have, Will," Nancy said. She was delighted to see her sister would be blessed with such a beautiful home and a man who loved her deeply. Nancy felt her sister was being rewarded for all the selfless and untiring dedication to her family and others.

"The Lord has been good to me," was Will's reply.

Betsy called for the women to come in for something to drink. She had a pitcher of her famous sweet tea waiting. The men unloaded the cars then joined them. Betsy was also anxious for Deborah to see the arbor. "Would you like to drink your tea on the high porch?"

"We'll drink it in the kitchen. The weather is a little warm today, so we'll relax inside," said Deborah. After they drank the tea, Deborah asked Will to show the house to Nancy and Jim.

Will was very proud of his home and got great pleasure showing it off. Deborah said she wanted to speak with Betsy to catch up on the final plans. Will seemed disappointed she wouldn't be accompanying them as he showed Nancy and Jim to the staircase to begin the grand tour.

Will chose to show the kitchen last so he could persuade Deborah to go with them to the garden. "Deborah, I want you to show Nancy where we plan to say I do."

"I would love to. Let's start with the high porch. It overlooks Will's amazing garden." Deborah led the way. She pointed out the various varieties of flowers and then directed them to look down the path to the two large magnolia trees. She explained they would be standing between them on

Saturday. It was then she spotted the arbor. "You had the arbor delivered."

"No, I decided to build it myself."

From the porch Deborah couldn't see the detail. She hurried down the stairs and forgot the others in her haste to take a better look at Will's handiwork. She stopped quickly when she could see the intricate detail. Deborah shouted, "Will, it's unbelievable. It looks like lace. How could you make it so detailed? It's incredible."

"I wanted to surprise you. It's one of your wedding gifts from me. Do you like it?"

"Like it, I'm awed by it. I didn't realize you had such talent. It's fantastic." Deborah seemed glued in place. Will joined her and put his arms around her and said, "I wanted something unique to remind us of our special day. I want to love and spoil you the rest of my life."

"I can't accept being pampered. I enjoy doing the spoiling."

Nancy hugged her sister. "I'm delighted to see you're getting what you deserve, the best of everything."

Betsy called from the porch to announce dinner was ready. Deborah realized this was just the beginning of a week filled with love. She was eager for Saturday's arrival.

Todd, Jamie, and the twins visited after dinner. Jamie was having difficulty walking. The baby was maneuvering herself for delivery, and it was an extremely uncomfortable time for her. Deborah asked, "Jamie, are you going to make it until Saturday?"

"The doctor has assured me it will be another two weeks, so I'm fairly confident I'll be attending the wedding."

"I'm sorry I put so much responsibility for the wedding arrangements on you at this time."

"It wasn't any trouble. I enjoyed the distraction, and the boys have been so excited about being in the wedding. They have been doing a penguin waddle since trying on their tuxedos."

The phone rang and it was Neal. He said Katie wasn't feeling well and promised Deborah they would stop by the next evening.

Everything was going extremely well. The caterer and florist guaranteed Deborah everything was on schedule and they would be at the house by seven in the morning on Saturday for setup. The photographer would come two hours before the ceremony to take the individual pictures; the arbor would be the backdrop for photos after the wedding. Betsy was taking care of the cake, and Deborah knew she could count on her for any glitches in the meantime.

Thursday's activities included picking up the tuxedos and alerting the hairdressers to be early for all the women. Neal brought Katie by for dinner, and Deborah was thrilled to see she was starting to show her pregnancy. Neal announced, "The baby's name is going to be Nathaniel." Everyone was delighted by the news they were having a boy.

Friday morning brought a flurry of activity. Todd went to the airport to get Donna, Ryan, Megan, Jason, and the girls. Robert and Susan had graciously offered to pick up Deborah's brother, Shawn, and his wife, JoAnne. Robert and Shawn would be officiating at the ceremony so it was convenient for them to plan the service.

Will's sister, Marilyn, would be staying with Katie and Neal. Marilyn was never fond of Deborah and felt Will shouldn't have dated her in high school. Deborah had spoken to her several times in the recent months and was looking forward to seeing her again. Marilyn mentioned Will convinced her he was content, and that's all she cared about.

Everyone arrived at the house by five o'clock for the rehearsal. They wanted to practice in the daylight. Deborah knew it would be futile after dark. With everyone assembled, they went to the garden and proceeded down the path toward the magnolias. Neal held Deborah by the hand and walked slowly to Will, who was beaming under the arbor. Deborah could sense this would be a very special ceremony.

They celebrated the rehearsal dinner at a nearby hotel. Deborah and Will looked at each other and marveled at the way the families had bonded. Will leaned over and whispered in her ear, "It won't be long and you'll be Debby Dougherty."

"I practiced writing that name over and over during my teen years."

Will laughed, and they enjoyed the rest of the evening with those closest to them.

Will left with Neal and Katie to spend the night at their home so Deborah could roam about the house without his interference on the big day.

Chapter Thirty-Four

S aturday's events began early. Todd was there to direct the caterers in setting up the chairs for the guests and placing the tables on the patio for the luncheon after the ceremony. The florist lined the path with white rose topiaries connected with white satin ribbon. A large blanket of white roses was placed on top of the arbor.

Betsy called Deborah to see the cake. She had decorated it with flowers and doves to match the design on the arbor. It was lovelier than Deborah could have imagined. "I hope you like it."

"Oh Betsy, it's better than any cake I've ever seen. You're special to us, and I want to thank you for all you do. Will and I have a present for you." Deborah reached into her robe pocket and handed Betsy an airline ticket. "Now take two weeks and visit with your sister in Florida. Will called and she's expecting you on Monday. It will give you tomorrow to pack, and Todd will take you to the airport."

"Deborah, thank you. I love you already."

"I'd better get dressed. The photographer will be coming, and I don't want to be late for my own wedding."

Deborah took the blue chiffon dress from the closet and stepped gently into it. She looked at her reflection in the mirror and smiled at the thought of being Mrs. William Dougherty. God does give you the desires of your heart, she thought. How he used the tragedies and turned them into triumphs. Her grandchildren would be near her in Atlanta, Neal was settled and looking forward to becoming a father, and Ryan was pursuing the ministry. All the transformations in such a short amount of time could only have been by God's design, but the most precious was the man God chose to enter her life once more. *How can I repay the Lord for all He has accomplished?* She gently placed the powder blue picture hat on and went to see if the others were ready. Nancy, Megan, Donna, and the children met her in the hallway. They all smiled their approval at seeing Deborah looking so radiant. The children were anxious to go downstairs. Her granddaughters looked very grown-up in their gowns, and the twins were doing their penguin walk; Deborah was proud of them all.

It was a gorgeous sunny day, the sky filled with white, puffy clouds. The musicians were setting up when Will arrived with Neal, Katie, and Marilyn. With the rest of the family assembled, the photographer began taking the individual groupings of men and women—taking extreme care that Will and Deborah didn't see each other before the ceremony.

The guests started arriving and taking their places in the garden.

The processional music began, and one by one, the wedding party slowly walked down the pathway. Will and Todd were waiting under the arbor with Shawn and Robert. As Neal and Deborah stepped out onto the white runner, Deborah could see Will. How handsome he looked. Her eyes focused on one man, a man she had waited a lifetime for.

Deborah was lost in his stare, and everything and everyone became hazy. She seemed to be floating on air.

Will took Deborah by the hand, and they stood facing each other. Shawn and Robert said some inspiring words, but Deborah didn't hear anything. She was waiting for the words that would make them man and wife. Will began his vows. It felt like a dream. She saw his mouth move, though nothing was reaching her ears. When Shawn turned to her, she knew it was her turn to repeat the vows. Somehow she got through it until she heard the words "I do" come from her lips. *Yes,* she thought, *it is really happening.* Robert announced, "You may kiss your bride."

Will took her in his arms and said softly, "Mrs. Dougherty, may I kiss you?" Then with the utmost tenderness, he pulled her toward him and kissed her gently. It was like he woke her from a dream. She could hear the applause of the guests seated just feet away. Their children and grandchildren gathered around them. Deborah couldn't release Will's hand. They were together now, for a lifetime.

Ushers escorted the guests to the tables for the reception, while some mingled in the garden. With the buffet served, Deborah and Will made their way to greet and thank each guest for coming. Then came the traditional wedding rituals. Deborah and Will stood before the cake lovingly prepared by Betsy. Will placed his hand on hers, and they cut through its dainty decorations. Deborah threw her bouquet, which was caught by Donna.

As the sun set, the guests began to leave. Will and Deborah took a few moments with each of their children, and then went into the house.

"Will, where are we going? Will you please tell me now?"

"Darling, we never finished our trip in Montana. We're going to Big Sky, but we are staying in Buckhead at the Ritz-Carlton tonight. Just pack an overnight bag, and we'll come back tomorrow morning for the rest of our luggage. Todd will take us to the airport."

"Are we staying at the same resort?"

"Not exactly—I'll tell you before we leave." Deborah was a little curious about his answer. He knew most of the resorts in the area, so she was sure he had made the best choice.

They pulled out of the driveway with everyone waving and wishing them well. The wedding had been everything she dreamed of, and now she was Mrs. Dougherty.

As the rest of the family gathered in the house to relax and reflect on the perfect day, Jamie started having contractions and knew she better contact the doctor. She was instructed to meet him at the hospital. Todd said it might be a false alarm and remarked Deborah and Will shouldn't be disturbed until they knew more. Everyone piled into their cars and followed Todd and Jamie to the hospital.

The doctor examined Jamie and felt she should remain for a few hours. The twins went home with Katie and Neal, and the rest of the family returned to their respective accommodations.

During the night, Jamie's water broke, so the doctor decided to induce her labor.

Todd knew his father and Deborah would want to know, so he phoned the hotel and left a message for them to call. Will woke early and saw the blinking light on the hotel phone. He didn't want to disturb Deborah but felt the message must be urgent for someone to try to reach them on their wedding night.

Will lifted the receiver and listened to the message. "Deborah, wake up."

"What's wrong?"

"We need to get to the hospital right away."

"What happened?"

"Jamie's gone into labor."

Deborah leaped out of bed and grabbed her bag. Just then the phone rang. Will lifted the phone and said, "Hello."

"Dad, I'm sorry to bother you, but we thought you might want to know Sherry just arrived."

"We were getting ready when you called. Congratulations! We'll be there as soon as we can to see little Sherry."

Deborah reached for Will. "Isn't it wonderful?"

Deborah reflected on the week after her reunion with Will and all the difficulties they faced. Today they were going to the hospital but for the best of reasons. The exciting news of becoming a new grandmother brought tears to her eyes.

"Are you feeling okay?"

"This has been the most extraordinary week of my life."

When they arrived, Shawn and Robert met them in the waiting room. Will asked, "How are Jamie and the baby doing?"

"They're both excellent," said Robert. "We came to be available to take you to the airport."

Will told them, "We want to visit with our granddaughter for a few minutes, and then we will meet you back at my house. We have to get our tickets and bags."

Jamie was holding the baby when they entered the room. She was smiling and held out the baby, wrapped tightly in a blanket, for Deborah to hold. "Sherry would like to see her grandmother."

Deborah reached to take the precious bundle. She looked down on the sweetest little face smiling back at her. "She's just beautiful."

Will put his hand on Deborah's neck and bent over her shoulder, peering down at the little blessing God had given. He remembered his son's separation and how this moment may have never happened. Will quietly thanked God for his family. He walked to the side of the bed and placed a kiss on Jamie's forehead. "Thank you for loving my son and being a special daughter."

Jamie eyes filled with tears as she embraced him. "You're the best dad ever."

"We won't be able to spend the time we would like because our plane will take off without us if we don't leave. Know we love you both and little Sherry, but I kept Deborah from enjoying Big Sky before, and I don't want her to be disappointed."

Todd said, "If it were my honeymoon, I'd feel the same way. We understand completely."

"Do we have to leave so soon?" Deborah playfully chided. She knew it would only be two weeks, but it was difficult to leave the newest member of the family.

While packing the extra items she would need for Montana, Deborah found her present for Will wrapped and tucked away in her suitcase.

Will entered the room. "Are you ready? I have something you'll need for our honeymoon." He handed her a box.

Inside held a key. "What's this for?"

"It's for our accommodations. I bought the cabin you liked in Montana. A decorator has furnished it for us, but you can make any changes you would like."

"Will, I can't believe it. What a wonderful present. Now, I also have a wedding gift for you." Deborah went to her suitcase and pulled out the wrapped package. It was marked, "With All My Love." Will took the paper off to reveal a book entitled *Reunion at Big Sky*. "Deborah, you finished your book. What a great surprise. I love it."

Will opened the novel, which held a bookmark in the dedication page. It read:

> To Will,
> God brought us together, and I will love you forever. It is my prayer we make many more memories at Big Sky.

Epilogue

With their gold medals tucked in their ski jackets and the rings just exchanged on their fingers, Alan and Beverly stepped from the tram and pushed off the mountain where it all began to embark on a journey that would last a lifetime.